MW00883458

Risk and Reward: An Erotic Halloween Novella

Aria Roselle

1

Risk and Reward: An Erotic Halloween Novella

Aria Roselle

Trigger and Content Warnings

This book contains some scenes that may be triggering for some readers. <u>This page does contain spoilers</u> but is an important read if you may have potential triggers. Following the list, there are more detailed explanations of the first two items for those who may need more information.

Trigger Warnings:

- Attempted rape
- Pill/opioid use
- Alcohol use
- Mild violence
- Consensual sex scenes involving the following: public play (both watching and participating), primal play, bondage, light knife play, and wax play.

*Attempted Rape: This book contains an instance of attempted rape of the main character as well as memories of an attempt from the past. Both scenes involve the same man and do not go further than him touching her upper body over clothing before she gets away. He does attempt to restrain her.

*Pill/Opioid Use: In one scene, characters competing in the challenge have to take a random pill of their choosing. One side character unknowingly takes an opioid and later experiences a sedative effect from it before panicking and leaving the party with a safe person.

CHAPTER ONE

I'M ALREADY REGRETTING this idea. With every step, the gravel crunches under our feet and I find myself wishing I had convinced Brooklyn to go somewhere else tonight. The two of us walk aside the long stretch of cars lining the edge of the street toward the farmhouse, its silhouette looming in the bright moonlight and the various Halloween-themed lights illuminating the front in shades of purple and orange.

The wind whips through the air, and I wrap my arms around myself. My skintight black bodysuit only offers so much protection against the chill, though I'm glad I decided on the one that covers me down to my wrists and ankles and fits me like a glove—the tiny one-piece Brooklyn had encouraged me to wear would have left most of my skin exposed and made me feel even more self-conscious here than I already do, not to mention put me at risk of freezing to death.

Okay, maybe that's a little dramatic, but still. It's fucking cold. Brooklyn, on the other hand, is all dolled up in a tiny latex dress with black and yellow stripes and bouncy antennas on top of her head, complete with a bright yellow clutch and black stilettos.

The cat ears on my head and the dramatic cat-eye makeup I spent too long perfecting might technically count as a costume, but realistically the only difference between my outfit tonight and my normal apparel is the presence of cat ears and a lack of other accessories. I even have on my trusty old Converse, not willing to put myself through the pain of heels, especially while I'm drinking.

I've always been a fan of the alternative style— fishnets, ripped clothing, chains, combat boots, heavy eyeliner, and lots of black—which isn't exactly the height of fashion in backwoods Kentucky and didn't do me any favors in terms of high school popularity. In this town, almost everyone fits the country vibe, so I always manage to stick out like a sore thumb. There's a reason I haven't been back in years.

As we approach the massive farmhouse, the faint thump of bass-heavy music grows louder, mingling with the sounds of laughter and chatter from inside. The place is packed. Brooklyn nudges me with her elbow, offering a reassuring smile. She knows how much I hate these kinds of events, but I promised her I'd be here this year. After three and a half years away at college and missing the last three Halloweens—our favorite holiday—, it feels like I owe her. We celebrated together every year growing up, trick-or-treating together, watching scary movies in her basement when we got too old to go out to collect candy, and stealing wine from her parents' stash when we were teens.

This is the first Halloween we've actually gone out partying together, and despite my aversion to being back in town, I'm glad to spend time with her. When she offered her spare bedroom to me for the weekend with the promise of horror movies, candy, and alcohol like old times, I couldn't say no.

The farmhouse is huge, with two stories and a wraparound porch that creaks under the weight of so many partygoers. The garish bright lights give a stark contrast to the darkness of the surrounding woods and the empty field across the gravel street behind us.

When we make it to the front door, a guy in a skeleton mask stops us. Brooklyn seems to know the drill, opening her wallet and handing the guy a twenty. "For both of us," she tells him. Then, turning to me, she says, "It's the least I can do to repay you for coming to the party with me." Skeleton guy has a clipboard and a cash box, which feels a bit more organized and official than I expected for a party in the middle of nowhere. They must want to make sure they cover the booze with entrance fees or something.

"Thanks," I mutter, trying to suppress the guilt of her paying for yet another thing for me this weekend. Brooklyn knows how tight money has been for me this year. Between student loans that barely cover tuition and the two jobs I juggle to pay for rent and food, every dollar counts.

"You girls taking the challenge?" the guy asks, his voice muffled by the mask.

"No," Brooklyn answers quickly, her tone firm. She grabs my arm and pulls me toward the door.

"What's the challenge?" I ask as soon as we step away.

She turns to me, leaning in close. "It's some messed up game they play every year at the Halloween party. I didn't stick around long enough for it last year." She shrugs and pulls me through the door into the chaos of the party.

Inside, the air is thick with the smell of alcohol, sweat, and a faint hint of weed. It doesn't seem much different than the one and only frat party I went to a couple years ago with the scents, the colorful lights, and the music drowning out every other noise..

A shiver runs down my spine—not from the cold, but from the uneasy feeling that always accompanies being back here. Rural Kentucky can be called a lot of things—some nicer than others—but exciting, accepting, and full of opportunity are not on that list of descriptors. Leaving for university was the best decision I ever made, and coming back for this party where I'm likely to run into old high school classmates feels like some sort of self-induced masochism. My head is on a swivel as we inch into the house.

Brooklyn leads the way, weaving through the crowd with ease. She's always been good at this—mingling, making friends, being the life of the party. She's one of those people who's popular with every group because she's genuinely kind to everyone. I'm grateful to have her as my best friend for all these years. Without her, I doubt I would've survived high school as relatively unscathed as I did.

The living room is packed, people crammed together on mismatched furniture and makeshift seating. A group of guys in various costumes—everything from a vampire to a half-naked cowboy to an inflatable t-rex—are playing beer pong in one corner. In another, a girl dressed as a gender-bent Beetlejuice is pouring shots from a bottle of something purple.

Brooklyn grabs my hand and pulls me toward the kitchen, where it's slightly less crowded. "Let the drinking commence!" she declares, rummaging through the assortment of bottles on the counter. She pours herself something bright red and hands me a bottle of my favorite beer.

I take the drink gratefully, leaning against the counter as I survey the room. It's a strange feeling being back here.

High school feels like a lifetime ago, though it's only been two and a half years. I was never really bullied—except by one girl that nobody particularly liked, but everyone kept on their good side because of her family's money and influence—but I certainly wasn't popular either. I got good grades, was cordial with the other students, and kept my head down. I suppose I could've made it easier on myself by dressing to fit in or forcing myself to join a club or sport, but that's just never been my style. I could never convince myself to be someone I'm not, even if it meant sacrificing social standing.

Brooklyn's chatting with a couple of guys that look somewhat familiar, her laughter cutting through the noise. That didn't take long. She's always been a social butterfly, but I can't help but feel a pang of envy. It's not that I want to be the center of attention, but sometimes I wish I was able to socialize so effortlessly like her.

"Sadie, you remember Ben and Josh, right?" Brooklyn's voice pulls me from my thoughts.

"Yeah, of course," I lie, offering a polite smile. I do vaguely recognize them, but I think they must have been a couple years ahead of us in school, because I would undoubtedly recognize anyone in our class and likely the ones directly above and below us as well. There's very little anonymity in small towns like this.

They nod in return and shoot off a quick greeting before returning their attention to Brooklyn, clearly more interested in her company than mine. I don't blame them. She has that easy sort of confidence that's almost magnetic, whereas my resting bitch face and nervous silence have the opposite effect. I've found a great group of friends in college, but coming back here seems to have reverted any feelings of confidence and security I might have gained.

I sip my beer, trying to ignore the knot of anxiety tightening in my stomach. I promised Brooklyn I'd be here, but being back in this environment feels disconcerting. Although, as I look around, I realize that I don't actually recognize many people. Weird. I would have expected a lot more of our old classmates to be around.

"Hey, you okay?" Brooklyn asks, pulling away from her conversation with the guys.

"Yeah, just... a little overwhelmed," I admit. I don't know what's wrong with me. I should be enjoying myself, especially now that I know there aren't too many people I went to school with, but the energy in the room is humming with a weird sort of tension that I can't quite place.

She grabs my hand and squeezes, offering a reassuring smile. "We can leave anytime you want, okay? Just say the word."

I nod, grateful for her understanding but knowing how disappointed she'll be if we leave early. "I'm just going to step outside real quick."

I manage to zig-zag through the crowd of people and make it to the door, the relief of the cold air a welcome change from the stifling heat inside. There's still a decent number of people hanging out on the porch, but most of the partygoers seem to be cramped inside.

Leaning against the railing, I stare out at the darkened field across the street and listen to the muted thump of bass coming from inside, and after a few minutes of standing there, I decide to explore.

I pass small groups of people congregated on the wraparound porch, quite a few huddled in and whispering conspiratorially. I absentmindedly wonder if there's some sort of drama happening.

When I reach the back of the house, I'm greeted by the sight of a massive bonfire in the back yard that makes the people standing next to it look tiny in comparison. Not quite ready to go in the house yet, I resume my position of propping my arms up on the railing and simply observing.

The sound of someone speaking close to me snaps me from my zoned-out state.

"Look who finally decided to show up to a party. It's been, what, six or seven years in the making?" My head snaps up, and I meet the gaze of someone I definitely recognize. Grant was not only one of the best players on our high school football team, but also was in the top ten of our graduating class. The typical all-American guy that everyone liked. We had a lot of the same classes, but we never really spoke.

"Haha, very funny," I answer.

"Why is that funny?" The look of genuine confusion on his face almost makes me laugh. Seriously?

"Because we both know that I wasn't ever invited to these things, especially not in high school."

His amused hazel eyes take in my expression. I know I'm not being very friendly, but I can't help but be on the defensive when it comes to guys like this. "Well, that wasn't by my choice."

I scoff. "Right. I'm sure you were dying to invite the weird goth girl to your shindigs."

"And what if I was?" he challenges, slipping his hands in his pockets. He's wearing jeans, an Aerosmith t-shirt, a leather jacket that hugs his body way too well, and aviators on top of his head.

"Then you should have done it back then."

"Touche."

"What are you supposed to be, anyway?" I ask, letting my eyes sweep over his outfit again.

"A rockstar." The corner of his mouth lifts. "And you're, what, a feisty kitty cat?"

I give him a deadpan stare, raising my eyebrows slightly. "I suppose."

Apparently, my standoffish tone does nothing to dissuade him, because he simply laughs. He rakes his hand absentmindedly through his brown hair, and I take the moment to appreciate his appearance, even if he's not my usual type. He's tall, with a sharp jawline, broad shoulders, and a lopsided smile. He

14

radiates easygoing confidence and has a naturally flirtatious air about him.

"Well, it's cute. I like it, even if you do seem to embody the feistiness a little too well."

Something about him makes me want to let my walls down, but I only allow myself to lower them a little. Being asked out as a joke so many times in my childhood and teenage years has done a number on me. There was one time I did go out on a date with a so-called "popular" guy who I was surprised had an interest in me, and it's a night I now try desperately to forget. I shudder at the memory of his wandering hands, his pushy attitude, and his aggressive persistence. If I hadn't lied about going to the restroom before sneaking out the back door and running home, things could have gotten much, much worse.

I return Grant's smile, mine much more guarded than his easy grin. "To be fair, I'm only here tonight because Brooklyn dragged me along."

"Oh yeah? Did she decide to take the challenge this year?"

I shake my head. "Not as far as I know. What is this challenge everyone keeps talking about, anyway? It seems like a big deal, but nobody can seem to explain to me what it actually is."

A wicked glint flashes in his eyes. "If you don't know, it's probably best I don't tell you. Especially since I'm just getting the chance to actually talk to you. Don't wanna scare you away just yet."

I cross my arms and stare at him expectantly, not falling for his boyish charm or flirtatiousness despite the traitorous butterflies fluttering in my stomach. I don't want to like him, but I can't help my body's response to his shameless gaze. There's a sort of magnetism to him that I'm finding hard to resist.

"Did you notice there aren't many people from high school here?" he asks.

"I did, as a matter of fact. What does that have to do with anything?"

"There's a reason only certain people know about this party. It's kept under wraps surprisingly well. And you know how hard it is to keep something a secret around here."

I nod. "And?"

"Well, that has to do with the challenge." He seems nervous all of the sudden, his thumb nail picking at the label on the bottle of beer he's holding and his eyes flicking side to side as people walk across the porch.

I sigh, my annoyance kicking up a notch. "You're just talking yourself in circles. What the hell is this big, secretive challenge?"

He's quiet for a moment, seemingly debating what to say. "Fine, I'll explain. But I'm warning you now, I don't know if you can handle it." He's still clearly nervous but manages to flash a teasing smile at me.

"Try me."

CHAPTER TWO

Grant glances over his shoulder to make sure no one's within listening distance before he speaks in a hushed tone. "Okay, so apparently the challenge started a few years ago as a sort of amped-up dare game. There was a big party here, everyone got drunk and started placing bets on people doing stupid shit, and it became an 'official' thing the next year where they planned out the dares or games in advance. It's just been growing each year."

"Interesting." I say nothing else, waiting for him to continue.

"So, that ten bucks you paid for an entrance fee goes into a pot. Whoever decides to take the challenge puts another ten in. The host takes two hundred of that, and the rest goes to the winner of the challenge."

I do a quick tally in my head. There has to be close to seventy people here, so the pot would at the very least be a few hundred dollars after the host takes out his share. That could be enough money to cover my food for a couple months if I stretched it . . .

"That's not all, though," Grant says, interrupting my thoughts about what I could do with a few hundred bucks. "Last year, once they got down to a certain number of players, each one got their own money bucket." He points toward the door, where there's a stack of Halloween candy buckets, each decorated in a different cheesy design of pumpkins, ghosts, candy, or monsters. "People use their money to vote on different participants, and the player gets to keep all the money they get. I think last year's winner ended up walking away with over a grand. Apparently a few of the guys save up quite a bit for this occasion."

Holy shit. A thousand dollars? Maybe I have questionable morals, but there's a lot of weird shit I'd do for that much money right now. I attempt to keep a neutral demeanor, but my heart and mind are already racing with the possibilities.

"So what's the actual challenge part then? The dares or games or whatever?"

His expression immediately drops into something more serious. "That's where it gets bad."

"Elaborate."

He looks over his shoulder again, his voice dropping a couple levels. "I'm really not supposed to be talking about it . . . but let's just say that shit gets dark real fast. Sex, humiliation, violence."

"Hmmm." Something about his expression tells me I should be running for the hills, but all he's done is intrigue me more. Could it really be that bad? How serious does it actually get? It's not like I'm a total stranger to kinky stuff, so it might all just be a matter of perspective.

"Don't tell me you're actually considering this."

"As much as I'd love to say I'm above humiliating myself a bit for money, I'm really not. Two grand could make a big difference for me right now."

"It's not worth it."

"No offense, but I don't think it's your place to tell me that. Not all of us got to go to college on football scholarships with wealthy, supportive parents on the sidelines."

He shakes his head softly. Whether it's in discouragement or resignation, I'm not sure. "You're right. But it doesn't matter anyway. This year you need a partner to play."

"Well, weren't you just saying you wished you'd gotten the chance to know me better? Here's your chance."

He raises his eyebrows. "You're serious?"

"Absolutely."

"What happened to that feisty, stay-away-from-me-or-I'll-cut-you attitude you had ten minutes ago?"

I give him a sly smile. "Maybe you've caught my attention for the time being. One more question, though. How do you win?"

"It's last person—well, couple—standing. I'm not really sure what happens if they run out of challenges and multiple people are still in it. Last year was the first year I actually came to this party, and I didn't even stick around until the end. I've just been telling you what I know from that. But I was only here for an hour after the challenge started, and six of the ten players dropped out by the time I left."

"So you can drop out whenever you want?"

"As far as I know."

"Hmm, I see." I weigh the pros and cons in my mind. Pros: I could win a lot of money, I might have fun, and I'll get to spend some more time with this admittedly attractive guy. Cons: I may embarrass myself, and it's likely I'll push myself too hard in order to win the money. But like he said, I can drop out whenever I want to, so what's the harm in trying?

"I'm in," I tell him. "Where do we sign up?"

He gives me another concerned look. "Are you absolutely sure?" He probably thinks I'm batshit insane by the expression on his face.

"Yes."

He chuckles at my resolute tone. "Then you're crazier than I thought. I'll find Cam and let him know to add us to the list."

A heady mix of fear and excitement rush through me as I watch him disappear into the house. What the hell am I getting myself into?

The next couple hours seem to happen in slow motion as I await whatever insanity the challenge will bring. It gives me enough time for my mind to start imagining all sorts of different disturbing scenarios. I have a couple drinks to quell my nerves, but I have a feeling I'm going to need to be fairly clear-headed for whatever is about to come.

"So, you said you're in college," Grant half-yells above the music. Despite the calmer atmosphere outside, it was too cold to stay out. "What are you studying?"

"Nursing," I tell him. I'm leaned in close so we can hear each other, though he has to lean down quite a bit to get his head closer to mine. "What about you?"

"I'm also planning on going into the medical field. The goal is to be a physical therapist, so I've got a few more years left."

Damn, okay, that's impressive. I was expecting him to say business or something.

Throughout our conversation, I learn that he's attending the school about an hour's drive from mine, he managed to snag a full scholarship for football, and he reads old science fiction novels in his spare time. We swap stories about school and our friends, and he catches me up on the never-ending small-town drama that's happened in the time since I've been gone. I guess he regularly comes back to visit his family, which is endearing.

I almost forget about the challenge, getting lost in my conversation with Grant, until the music ceases abruptly and the room goes quiet.

"The challenge will begin in ten minutes at the stroke of midnight," a man announces from the back doorway. "If you're participating, please head out to the back porch. If you're not participating, I'd still encourage you to come out to watch."

The room is silent for only a second before the music resumes, quieter than it was before, but the carefree chatter has now morphed into whispers and the occasional nervous laugh. Most of the people in the room are shuffling toward the door.

I look up at Grant, who's already staring down at me.

"Ready?" He asks.

"Yep. Real theatrical of them to do it at the stroke of midnight," I muse, hoping he doesn't notice the waver in my voice. Anxiety gnaws at my stomach as we join the throng of people filtering outside, but I keep my head held high. Maybe it's for show or maybe it's because he can sense the worry buzzing through me, but Grant slips his hand in mine as we step away from the crowd and line up next to the other couples who are lined up against the railing of the back porch next to the man with the clipboard from earlier.

I don't know if it makes me feel better or worse that most of the others look just as nervous as I feel. Eyes flit back and forth as everyone surveys their competition. By the time all of us are lined up, the tension in the air is tight and humming with nervous anticipation. The atmosphere of the party has shifted to something frenetic and slightly foreboding.

The man with the clipboard—who Grant tells me is Cam, the guy who lives here and organizes the party—is wearing a full ringmaster costume, complete with a top hat, a bright red tailcoat, and a bowtie. He commands everyone's attention. "First things first, some things will be different about this year's challenge. Starting with this."

I squint, trying to figure out what he's holding up as a few chuckles sound around me.

"After Lucy's stunt last year, we need to make sure you're not too drunk to play. The last thing we need are medical emergencies or the cops showing up."

There's another round of laughter and some nods of agreement.

While Cam makes his way from player to player, making each do the breathalyzer before moving on, I take the time to check out my competition, though I'm still not exactly sure what sort of competing we'll be doing. There are only ten couples, and I'm surprised more people don't volunteer to compete with how much money is on the line.

Cam steps over to the next couple once he's satisfied with the reading on the breathalyzer for the last. But when the man pulls off his mask, my blood runs cold.

It's him.

Flashbacks of that night a few years ago flicker through my mind—the way he kept encouraging me to drink too much, the way his hands roamed even when I told him to stop. A shudder runs through me, made even worse when he steps aside and reveals the woman on the other side of him. Kyla. She was pure evil in high school, taking pride in making people's lives miserable if she deemed them as lesser than, which was a lot of us. She took a particular liking to picking on me for my unconventional style choices. She's currently dressed as a princess—I think—with her short, tight, sparkly pink dress and a tiara. Either that or a beauty pageant contestant.

Maybe she's changed, I tell myself, even though I know deep down that it's bullshit. The man she's partnered up with tells me everything I need to know about her character.

I was already nervous about the challenge, but the idea of potentially interacting with either one of them has dread coiling in my gut.

The chatter continues around us, seeming louder than it did a moment ago, and when Cam walks up to us, we dutifully blow into the breathalyzer. He gives each of us a thumbs up and moves on to the last two couples.

I'm turning to tell Grant about my concern about Mason and Kyla when I catch a familiar face staring at me in the crowd. Oops, I guess I got so caught up in my conversation with Grant that I forgot to tell Brooklyn about joining the challenge.

Brooklyn looks equal parts shocked and worried for me. I wave at her, but she just raises her arms, palms upward, as if to ask, what the hell are you doing? I lift my hand and rub my thumb, pointer finger, and middle finger together in a gesture that tells her exactly why I'm doing this—money.

She shakes her head at me, to which I respond with a reassuring smile. I hope it looks convincing, because it's entirely fake. How can I reassure her when I'm brimming with anxiety?

Cam makes his way to the front of the crowd, near the steps of the porch, and clears his throat, his eyes sweeping over us. "Alright, everyone," he starts, his voice cutting through the noise and somehow making the situation feel even more eerie. "The challenge is about to begin."

He taps his fingers against the clipboard in a steady rhythm as the noise dies down to an unsettling hush. I glance around, my nerves twitching. Twenty-somethings at a Halloween party should be loud, obnoxious, and careless. Instead, there's this unsettling sort of quiet, like the calm before the storm.

My heart skips a beat. I still don't know what I've signed up for, and the suspense is gnawing at me. My costume feels suddenly too tight, too revealing as it clings to my skin. The glow of cheap orange Halloween lights and the yellowish overhead porch lights casts long shadows across the yard that make everything seem more ominous.

"As some of you know," Cam continues, his voice measured, "a few select people are allowed to submit challenges for consideration, and I pare them down into a list. Then, I put them in order for the night. My party, my rules." He smirks. "So, let's lay down some ground rules."

Everyone is silent. With the tension in the air and all eyes on us, this feels like a trap I've walked into willingly.

"Number one, and most important," Cam says, his tone turning serious. "If a participant says 'Stop,' 'No,' or any variation of that expressing their lack of consent or desire to stop, whatever is happening immediately ends, and they forfeit the challenge."

That should be comforting, but it isn't. Instead, it only reminds me that I have no idea what kind of fucked up games would require a rule like that.

"Rule number two," Cam continues, "if you get caught with your phone out during any of the challenges, whether you're playing or watching, you're getting kicked out, and will probably get the shit beat out of you on the way out. This whole thing needs to stay a secret, and if videos start floating around, the cops will be on our asses."

My anxiety ratchets up another notch.

"Now, for those of you who haven't done this before," Cam says, and his eyes land on me for a moment before skimming over the rest of the participants, "the 'challenge' is a mix of different games and competitions. Some you need to win—or at least not lose—, and some just require participation without dropping out. This porch will serve as a sort of 'home base' for most of these challenges."

I nod, though I'm not sure he notices. My mind is racing through all the possibilities. Grant did tell me that there'd be sexual aspects and some humiliating circumstances, but how far does that go?

"The old rule," Cam says, a mischievous grin spreading across his face, "was that participants get to keep whatever money they have in their bucket once they drop out. However, that's changing this year."

A ripple of surprise goes through the spectators. Cam continues, "This year, the winner gets to keep all the money from everyone's buckets."

Gasps and whispers break the quiet as heads turn and eyes widen, especially amongst the players. Even I can't help but feel a jolt of surprise. How much money could that be? Enough to matter, obviously, given the reactions. Enough to make a difference. I think about my student loans, my crappy part-time jobs, the constant stress of making ends meet. That money would be more than just an exciting win for me; it would be a lifeline. I'm sure I'd have to split the money with Grant, but even then it sounds like it would be a significant amount. If the winner last year got over a thousand, this will probably be at least double.

But at the same time, unease spreads through me. If the money is so much higher, the stakes probably are too. Threads of hope and fear intertwine and snake through my body.

"As a bonus," Cam adds, "everyone gets a money bucket this year, instead of just the final five."

Cam grabs the pile of Halloween candy buckets and hands them down the line to each of us. I can't help but picture money piling up in each one, only for me to take them all at the end of the night.

"A.J. and I will be the designated money counters." Cam gestures to the man standing near him who flashes two thumbs up to the group. "And if you need change for bills or want to get cash, go see Jimmy. He'll take Venmo for cash, too."

There's a shuffle as a few people head over to where Jimmy sits with a heavy-duty lockbox. I recognize him from his earlier post at the front door, noticing the skeleton mask now sitting on the top of his head rather than covering his face.

"This feels weirdly official," I murmur to Grant.

"That's because it is. This is the party of the year. It's a big deal for some of these people, and shit's about to get really weird really fast."

Cam's voice cuts through again. "Remember, your money is your vote, and whichever lovely couple wins this will deserve every bit of it. Good luck to everyone," he says, sizing up each of us lined up before him. "You're gonna need it."

CHAPTER THREE

"SO, IS THERE a reason he's the host?" I whisper to Grant while we wait for our next directions. I can tell Cam is probably a few years older than we are and, by the looks of it, knows practically everyone here.

"From what I've heard, he and his friends were the ones who started this whole thing a few years ago, and he's been hosting it ever since. His parents are pretty old and have some issues, so they gave him the house while they went off to some assisted living place, I guess. So he's able to host this party every year because of that. As for why he does it, I think he just likes the chaos." Grant shrugs. "I don't know him that well, but a couple of my friends do, and they say he and his buddies are the type to push limits as far as they can and then go a little further. He's a nice guy as far as I can tell, but I definitely think he's got a dark side, and being able to push people past their limits for money seems to give him a bit of a God complex."

"Interesting," I say. "I don't think that makes me feel any better." I try to say it as a joke, but it falls flat because we both know it's a real concern. How far will he try to push things? And the better question is, will I be complicit by continuing to play the game?

Cam takes his place facing the crowd and announces the next challenge. "This first challenge will be pretty easy . . . probably." He grins, knowing full well that he's lying. "We recruited quite a few people to make cards with different dares or challenges on them. It's pretty simple, really. Each of you picks a card and completes the dare. No swapping cards, no alternatives."

"So what happens if you don't do the dare?" someone asks.

"Then you're out of the game," Cam says matter-of-factly, as if it isn't a big deal for someone to drop out of a competition where we could potentially win thousands of dollars. Hell, it may be just fun for some of them, but I really need that money. I'm in this shit to win it.

Cam pulls a deck of playing cards out of his pocket, shuffles them, and spreads them across the table in one smooth arc. "These each have your task written on the face side. Some of them have monetary prizes as well. Choose wisely."

We each go up as a pair, picking our cards before hurrying back to our places. Every couple is already whispering to each other, some laughing and some looking worried.

My heart races as Grant and I lock eyes before lifting our cards to read them silently, a wave of anxiety washing over me before dissipating.

I let out a sigh of relief when I read mine.

Grant flashes his card to me as soon as I'm done reading my own. "Swap shirts (and bras, if applicable) with one of the other participants."

Conveniently, Cam chooses Grant to go first, likely due to his unbothered expression. Grant reads the card aloud for everyone to hear then looks around, his gaze landing on the guy closest to his size. "I guess it's your lucky night," he jokes, already pulling off his leather jacket and lifting the hem of his shirt.

"Jacket too," Cam says when Grant looks over at him questioningly.

The other guy—who is dressed as a pirate—sighs and removes his shirt, which is a flowy black long-sleeved top with a criss-cross tie over the chest. "I want that back before the end of the night," he warns Grant.

"Likewise. That's my favorite jacket." Grant pulls the shirt over his head and adjusts the cinched sleeves then turns to me. "How do I look?" He asks, holding out his arms.

"Weirdly hot, actually."

He chuckles and shakes his head as Cam instructs me to read my card.

"From now until the next challenge, you must kneel at the feet of your partner, and you're not allowed to speak. If you break these rules, you have to give fifteen dollars of your money to someone else." As soon as I finish the sentence, I lower myself to the ground at Grant's feet, sitting next to him like a loyal little pet. It might be humiliating for some people, but I feel perfectly happy here. I sit back on my haunches and lean my head against his thigh, and his hand smoothes over my hair, making sure to avoid the clipped-in cat ears.

"Such a good little kitty," he murmurs, and I flip him off as I glare up at him but can't help the smile that peeks through.

I stay on my knees observing the other players' challenges from my place on the ground. One guy gets a card that instructs him to give his phone to the person to his left and let them go through it. Of course, the guy he gives it to immediately finds his girlfriend's nudes, which she's obviously pissed about. One of the girls gets a card for a mini beer pong challenge where she has to make three cups before the person she chooses to play against. She loses and has to forfeit ten dollars to the girl who beat her.

Another guy's card tells him to make out with two people that aren't his partner for thirty seconds each. His eyes pass over me, making my heart stop in its tracks, before he ultimately chooses Kyla and one other girl in some sort of anime costume. Being on the ground next to a big, strong man has its advantages, apparently.

The tension continues to ramp up with each card. Some are more sexual, like the guy taking a body shot of tequila off of his partner while the rest of us watch him lick the salt from her stomach then take the lime from between her lips, and some are more physically demanding, like the silly push-up competition.

Finally, the last of the couples is up—Kyla and Mason. Mason goes first, reading his card aloud. "Pick someone of your own gender to wrestle with.

First person to tap out gives ten dollars to the winner. No punching, hitting, or kicking."

Mason's eyes skim the players and, as expected, he chooses the smallest guy here. "You." He points.

Everyone either goes on the grass beside them or leans up against the porch railing to watch as Mason and his opponent go out into the yard. I crawl alongside Grant and peer through the thin wooden posts. When Cam calls out the start of the match, it takes all of ten seconds for Mason to have the poor guy's arm twisted behind his back with his face in the dirt. The guy struggles and tries to fight back, but he's overpowered and outweighed by probably sixty pounds and quite a few inches of height.

"You win, you win!" He shouts as Mason digs a knee into his back. Mason gives a smug smile before pulling back even harder. There's a sickening popping sound, and Mason finally lets go.

The guy shouts in pain and grabs his shoulder with his opposite hand. "You motherfucker," he spits. "You did that on purpose!"

Mason shrugs, seeming completely unaffected. "It was an accident, sorry." There's absolutely no way that was an accident, and anyone that knows him would realize that. The cruel, smug look on his face makes it even more apparent.

Mason makes his way onto the porch, unbothered by the pained sounds the other man is making, and when the guy comes up onto the porch, his shoulder seems to be hunched forward. He breathes through clenched teeth as his partner inspects it.

"I think it's dislocated," she says, panic lacing her voice.

A couple guys from the crowd step up. "We can probably pop it back into place. Here, let's go inside."

Grant and I flash each other worried looks, knowing that a couple half-drunk guys probably shouldn't be trying to fix a dislocated shoulder. It's out of our hands, though.

"Last up!" Cam exclaims. All eyes turn to Kyla.

She holds up her card and reads it. "Choose a player to race to the tree line and back. The loser gives the winner ten dollars."

"Who's it gonna be, then?"

Her eyes snap to me. "Sadie."

Of fucking course. I sigh and stand, but as soon as I'm on my feet, her head swivels back to Cam.

"She broke the rules of her card by standing up! Doesn't that mean she's disqualified?" She crosses her arms expectantly.

"Since it was overruled by another card, no. She's fine."

Kyla huffs and I flash her a feigned friendly smile. She probably only chose me for the sole purpose of hoping to get me disqualified, but she's totally screwed herself now, and I get a smug sense of satisfaction watching her face drop when she realizes it. She's wearing pointed heels with her short, tight dress while I've got on my Converse and a comfortable stretchy outfit. Lucky for her, one of her friends quickly switches shoes with her so that she's got flip flops instead of heels.

I'm still not exactly a fast runner, but I have a decent shot at winning this. We follow Cam's directions as he leads us out into the grass, designating one of the jack-o-lanterns as the starting and finish line and pointing to a massive tree across the yard that we'll have to circle before running back. Easy enough.

"Ready, set, go!"

Kyla and I take off, and the cold night air fills my lungs as I sprint toward the tree. Kyla's close behind, and I can hear the flopping sound of her shoes with each step. It doesn't take long for us to reach the tree, and we both slow slightly to loop around it.

But before I can start picking up speed for the last stretch, something hits the side of my shin, and I stumble a bit as Kyla's foot pulls away from me. Seriously? I guess she and Mason are a match made in hell with the violence and sabotage.

She's only a few steps ahead of me as I pick up my pace, but the anger fuels me, pumping blood through my veins and giving me that final push I need. I pass her halfway through the yard, my body getting into the groove of long, quick strides. When I pass the jack-o-lantern a couple seconds before Kyla does, I'm met with cheers and claps, and Grant lifts me and spins me around, making butterflies erupt in my stomach.

"That was fucking awesome!" He praises as he sets me down.

Remembering the instructions of my card and unsure if I'm free from all of them or just the standing portion of the rule, I choose to play it safe. I give Grant a massive smile before making the motion of zipping my mouth shut, reminding him.

"Got it," he says, immediately understanding. "Better safe than sorry."

Kyla's glare burns into me as Cam transfers ten dollars from her bucket to mine, but I ignore it. She can be pissed all she wants, but she brought this on herself.

Cam announces that Mason's wrestling opponent has decided to withdraw from the game, meaning his partner has as well. I do feel bad for him, but that's also one less competitor for me.

But now my desire to win is twofold; I need that money, but I'd love nothing more than to kick Kyla's ass at any challenges thrown our way tonight.

Feeling a renewed sense of purpose and a fire burning deep inside me, I look expectantly at Cam, ready for whatever fucked up games he's prepared next.

CHAPTER FOUR

"LOOKS LIKE THAT completes challenge one," Cam announces. "Nine couples are still in it to win it. So, let's get on to the next." He looks down at his clipboard as the crowd of people wait eagerly for the next wild bit of entertainment.

His lips lift in a smile when he reads off the item. "Lap dances." The crowd cheers, and Cam waves his hands around to shush them. "Here are the rules: Each guy gets a chair to sit in, and each girl has to give her best lap dance. Everyone's buckets will be out in front of them, so for those of you watching, remember to throw in money as your vote. This will last five minutes. The couple with the least amount of money at the end of the timer will be eliminated."

Shit. I glance up at Grant, who's already looking down at me with raised eyebrows. "Just remember, you can drop out any time you want. You're in charge here," he adds, trying to lighten the mood.

I shake my head. "No, it's okay. I'll do it." What's the harm in a little bit of humiliation when so much money is on the line?

Cam and his buddies line up chairs along the porch, where the guys each sit. I and the other women stand next to them, waiting for our cue. Glancing over at the couples to my sides, I notice the girl next to me looks just as nervous as I feel. A few seats down, I see Mason leaning back, hands behind his head with a sleazy grin on his face. What a douchebag.

"Alright, five-minute timer starts now."

A sultry, sexy song comes over the speakers. We all stand there for a split second, afraid to start, until Kyla makes the first move and stands in front of Mason before dropping down and rubbing her ass against his crotch.

Ew.

I pull my attention away from them and focus on the task at hand. Okay, Sadie, you can be sexy. You're wearing a skintight bodysuit and cat ears, for Christ's sake.

Instead of following the moves of all the other girls, I swing around behind Grant's chair and lean over slowly, running my hand from his shoulder down his chest and abdomen, stopping at his waistband before dragging my hand back up. His head turns slightly to the side toward me, and I try to ignore the pleasant chills that creep up my spine from his breath on my neck. Focus, Sadie.

I swing around the chair to the front of Grant, swaying my hips slowly to the music. His eyes darken as they move down my body, taking in my tight outfit.

Moving with more confidence now, I arch my back and run my hands through my hair as I dip low. Whistles and shouts sound around us, and a feeling of

39

power surges through me, knowing I have not only have his full attention, but the attention of quite a few other people watching from the crowd. His hands graze my waist as I bend forward and brush against him, my ass in his lap.

"That's it," he murmurs. "Just like that." I would think he'd be saying that to add to the showiness of all this, but he says it quietly enough that I know it's only for me. His tone now is lower, entirely different from his casual flirtation earlier, and it's sexy as fuck.

His words send a thrill through me, and I find myself enjoying this a lot more than I anticipated.

I can feel Grant's body responding to my movements, and I let a smirk slip onto my face. This may be just for show, but it's definitely turning me on more than I thought it would, and apparently him too.

Out of the corner of my eye, I notice dollar bills landing in the bucket near Grant's feet. The crowd is loving our show—not too much more than the others', but enough that I know we aren't getting eliminated, at least not this round. I turn my back to the crowd and bend over, leaning in close to Grant, my lips just barely grazing his ear.

"This is kind of fun," I whisper.

"I can't complain either." There's still a hint of playfulness in his voice, but also an edge to it that wasn't there before.

Feeling emboldened, I flip my hair before placing my hands on his shoulders and straddling his lap. His jaw clenches as I grind my hips against him in slow but exaggerated movements. Okay, fuck. This is hot. The fabric between us is thin enough for me to feel his erection against my thigh, and we're close enough that I can hear the hitch in his breathing when I move a certain way. When his eyes connect with mine, electricity seems to shoot between us, jarring but not unwelcome.

The spell is broken when the music cuts off and Cam announces, "That's the end of the challenge!" Again, the tension returns as we wait for Cam and A.J. to count the money from each bucket. They do it in front of everyone, and A.J. writes each number down on the clipboard. When they get to us, we're the second-to-last couple in the line and I've made sure to remember the lowest number I've heard so far, which is twenty-one dollars. My eyes are trained on the cash in Cam's hand, and relief floods me when he counts past that number with quite a few bills left in his hand. We total out at forty-four bucks, which is not the highest of the group but still on the upper end.

It only adds fuel to my fire. I—we—could win this thing. I'm practically buzzing with anticipation waiting for Cam to count the last couple's money, and when he does, he makes the announcement of who received the lowest and is therefore kicked out. They're people I don't know, but they both frown and disappear into the house. Guess they're not sticking around to watch the rest.

A.J. confiscates their money bucket and slips the few bills into a large manila envelope labeled "Challenge" before tossing the bucket to the side.

"Competitors, don't get too comfortable yet." Cam has another wicked smile on his face, looking every bit the eccentric ringmaster, and the noise dies down to a low hum of voices. I turn my head in his direction, looking past the line of most of the contestants aside from the one couple remaining on our other side at the end of the line, and I catch Mason's eye. Fuck.

His lips lift upward in what's probably supposed to resemble a smile, but it only reminds me of an animal baring its teeth, ready to strike. Dread coils in my guy as I snap my eyes away from him. How I didn't realize what a sleazy piece of shit he was before I went out on a date with him, I'll never know.

I try to shake the feeling of unease and focus my attention back to Cam, who is giving the next challenge.

As he reads off the stipulations from the clipboard in his hand, my jaw drops. "Each female must give their partner a blowjob. This one will also be on a timer, and if you can manage to finish him off, there's an extra fifty going into your cash bucket."

He can't be serious, right? Is there a designated person to check whether the guy comes or not? Is this a joke? I look over at Grant for confirmation, and he's giving me the same look as before—a mix of amusement and questioning of do you really want to do this?

"So, I hope your ladies' dances were enough to help your guys get it up," Cam continues, and snickers resound through the crowd of spectators. "We'll move you over here—" he gestures to the grassy area that's off the porch and directs the men to line up against the raised railing while the women wait on their knees in front of them.

This is so fucking demeaning, I think as my knees hit the wet grass and the dew starts to skink through the thin fabric. But it's worth it, I remind myself. We just have to win. I don't allow myself to think of what other fucked up scenarios they might put us through later tonight.

I glance up at Grant, embarrassment flooding through me because I probably should have asked him if he was okay with this. Though I suppose if he didn't stop me beforehand, he must be. Not to mention that his erection has hardly gone down since the lap dance, from what I can see. I also can't say that I'm not a little turned on by the idea of sucking him off, even here in front of everyone.

We're slightly more obscured than we would have been up there, but not much, and we're especially visible to those who can manage to get an overhead view from the railing.

We follow Cam's direction, but one couple stays on the porch, whispering to him and handing over their bucket before stepping back to join the people watching.

"Looks like we're down to seven couples now. You all get another five minutes for this challenge. Make it count. I have the buckets lined up here behind each of you for tips, but nobody will be voted out this round. This is just for fun."

His last statement is met with cheers and clapping, though those of us lined up in the grass are silent. "Oh, and no music this time," he adds. Great, so everyone gets to hear the sounds of seven sloppy blowjobs happening at once.

I don't even realize I'm avoiding Grant's eyes until his fingers graze the underside of my chin and lift it so I'm staring up at him.

"Relax," he murmurs. "You don't have to do anything you don't want to do."

I blow out a breath. "Okay. I'm alright, just nervous for some reason."

"Just keep your eyes on me. Nobody else matters right now."

Feeling strangely comforted by his words, I nod and answer, "Okay," just as Cam counts down. "Three, two, one . . . go!"

There's a sound of zippers being pulled down and clothes shuffling on either side of us, but my gaze is trained on Grant. He slowly reaches down and unbuttons his jeans before pushing down the front of his waistband.

His cock is hard and thick, springing out of his boxers. Damn it, is there anything about this man that isn't perfect? He stands there, staring down at me and waiting for me to make the first move.

I raise myself up on my knees and take him in my mouth slowly, letting my tongue flick over the head of his cock before suctioning my lips around him and easing down inch by inch.

In my peripheral vision, I notice people shoulder to shoulder on the porch, peeking over trying to get a good look. A few hoot and holler, making lewd jokes and laughing at themselves, but I don't let it bother me. In fact, the thought of them watching only spurs me on more. If I'm going to suck dick in front of a bunch of drunk assholes, I'm going to do a damn good job of it.

There's a commotion a ways down from us followed by someone walking back up onto the porch a minute later, and I'm assuming someone else dropped out, but I don't have time to dwell on that right now.

Normally, I'd take my time during a blowjob by teasing and building up the tension, but we're on a time limit, and I'm here to win. I suck him hard, base to tip then back again, and his head tilts back as he lets out a soft groan. I take that as all the encouragement I need, continuing my rhythm of bobbing my head up and down on his cock and using my tongue to give the head extra attention.

"Fuck, that feels so good," he says, his voice soft enough for only me to hear. He smoothes a hand over my hair and rests it at the back of my head, pushing me toward him as he thrusts his hips forward, gently fucking my throat. I reach a hand up and circle it tightly around the base of his cock. My hand massages him firmly as I take him deeper into my mouth, matching his thrusts as we build a steady rhythm. His thigh tenses under my other hand where I'm holding myself steady, his breath quickening.

I glance up at him and he's already staring down at me, his eyes hooded and dark with lust. I maintain eye contact even as my eyes water as I take him over and over again. I'm hit with the sudden realization that we're being watched, having been so caught up in the moment that it felt like only me and him for a moment. The fact that others can see me pleasuring him like this, all messy and desperate, sends a spike of arousal through me.

I move faster, sucking him with abandon now as he grips my hair tighter. My lips drag up and down his hard length as I swirl my tongue over the swollen head. A grunt escapes his lips and his hips buck as he pushes himself deeper into my mouth. With the way his thrusts become more erratic, I know he's getting close. I squeeze my thighs together, desperate for a little bit of friction with how turned on I'm getting by watching him and feeling him.

I'm aware of a presence behind us somewhere, but I don't let it slow me down.

"I'm going to come," Grant warns me, his voice low and husky, and I keep up with the pace he sets with the pulsing of his hips until the salty taste of his cum hits my tongue, and I swallow him down eagerly. His eyes shut and his chest heaves with heavy breaths as I suck down every drop. When I'm done, I lean back and pull my hands away from his body. He smiles down at me and offers me his hand. I take it and stand, and he zips his pants back up.

When I turn around, I see Cam watching from ten feet away. He simply gives us a thumbs up and checks off a box on his clipboard. Fucking weirdo.

Grant and I head back up to the porch and are greeted with cheers from the people who just watched me suck his dick. Is it weird that I feel a little proud of myself?

We lean up against the wall, not caring to watch the rest of the participants as the timer ticks down. I do notice that one of the couples is gone now, which must have been what the commotion was about. When Grant asks one of his friends what happened, he laughs and says, "He couldn't even get it up, so he got embarrassed and gave up. His girl seemed pissed."

That does suck for them, no pun intended, but they also could have kept trying. Cam did say there were no eliminations this round, only tips. Speaking of tips . . .

I inch my way through the people clustered up on the porch and peek inside our bucket. Damn, that's looking better every round. It's hard to tell how much is in there, but we're only halfway through the night—at least, I think we're about halfway through—and I'd guess there's a hundred in there, minimum. If that's doubled and then combined with everyone else's winnings, we could easily walk away with even more money than I expected.

But the challenges will only get worse from here, and I can only wonder how much of my morals I might have to set aside as the night goes on. I can't get cocky, because I have no clue what comes next.

CHAPTER FIVE

My stomach is in knots as we make our way back onto the porch, an odd thrill of pride, excitement, and fear of what's next coursing through me. Each challenge has been more intense than the last, and there are still six couples left in the game. I imagine there are at least a few challenges left before this is over.

The energy of the party tonight has morphed into something that's becoming darker by the minute, like everyone is hungry for more because tonight is the night to let go and let out those carnal, depraved urges.

Cam, looking as unbothered and mischievous as ever, takes his spot in front of everyone. "Okay, this next challenge is going to be interesting—me and they guys spent a lot of time talking this one out." My heart feels like it's about to pound out of my chest. Grant slips his hand in mine and squeezes, which calms me down slightly. He's in this with me, I think. I'm not doing this alone.

"Here are the rules. Each female player is going to get a head start to run off into the woods back there." He points to the darkened area straight across the yard where the tree line starts. "Guys, your job is to find your woman and bring her back here." Okay, seems straightforward enough.

"However—" he pauses for dramatic effect "— there is a chance to swap partners." A rumble of shock goes through everyone, heads turning and voices whispering excitedly. Those of us competing in the challenge mostly look warily at each other. My heart stops when I see Mason staring at me with malice and determination in his eyes. Oh fuck.

"Here's how that works. As long as one guy and one girl cross the finish line together, that will be their new pairing the rest of the night. If you catch her, you keep her. Same rules apply as before, guys— you can bring her here however you want, but if she says "stop," she forfeits the competition and you need to stop whatever you're doing and find someone else. Everyone good so far?"

Heads nod. My skin prickles in awareness, feeling eyes on me. I don't need to look around to know whose they are.

"Good. The woods back there are very dark, but there's a fence around the perimeter of the property, so if you happen to get lost, just keep walking in any direction until you find the fence and then follow it back here. This challenge will last for one hour, and if you're not back with a partner by the time the clock runs out, you're out of the game. We have a couple big ass fireworks here that we'll set off to signal when it's over if anyone's still out there."

"Any questions?" Silence. "Great. You have two minutes to discuss with your partner, starting now."

I turn to Grant, and before he can say anything, I blurt, "Mason is going to try to get to me first. We can't let that happen." I can hear the panic in my own voice, but I don't have time to explain the situation to him.

"Okay," he says, his voice resolute barely above a whisper so nobody else hears our plan. "Here's what I want you to do. When you get to the tree line, walk straight back two hundred steps. Walk, don't run, and keep your steps as normal as you can. Then turn right and walk one hundred steps that way. Find a tree or something to hide behind. I'll start calling out your name when I get close."

"Got it." I twist my hands in front of me in an attempt to keep them from shaking.

Grant gently squeezes my shoulders with his large hands. "Sadie, look at me."

I look up at his face, trying to keep my breathing even and my panic under control.

"I won't let him hurt you. I got you." There's something about the determination in his eyes and the reassurance in his voice that calms me down, if only a little. Maybe I'm crazy, but I believe him.

"Ladies, your five-minute head start begins now!" Cam yells, blowing an air horn.

We run.

The six of us sprint toward the woods, a few veering off to the left and right. I run straight back, but I slow once I hit the tree line. I need to be smart about this. My heart beats against my ribcage and I can hear my pulse pounding in my ears. Thankfully, I have an easier outfit to run in than most of these women, even if it was entirely unintentional. The outfit clings to my body, making it easy to move, with the black fabric adding a layer of camouflage for me in the darkness.

The darkness consumes everything as I begin walking, making sure to count my steps. I'm forced to go slowly, feeling out each step as I'm unable to see where my feet are landing.

I keep counting, step by step, as the blackness of the night closes in around me. My breaths are shallow, and I try to quiet them, afraid they'll give me away. The woods are silent except for the crunch of leaves beneath my feet and the distant sounds of laughter and music from the party that fade with each inch further into the woods. Every shadow seems to move, every rustle feels like it's drawing me closer to danger.

Twenty-seven, twenty-eight, twenty-nine. I count in my head, focusing on the numbers to keep calm as my eyes adjust only slightly to the darkness.

When I reach two-hundred, I turn directly to my right and hope I've been able to keep my path straight with all my stepping over branches and around shrubbery. I restart my counting.

One, two, three . . . That five minute head start is likely ending by now, if it hasn't already. They're coming for us.

My steps quicken.

I freeze, hearing a twig snap to my right, and I twist my head in the direction of the sound. My heart leaps into my throat. I pause, holding my breath, trying to listen over the pounding of my heart. My eyes scan the darkness, looking for any sign of movement even though it's practically impossible to see anything anyway.

Nothing. I exhale slowly and continue moving forward, one cautious step at a time.

Fifty, fifty-one, fifty-two. Almost there.

When I hit one-hundred, I take in my surroundings and decide to duck behind a massive oak tree, its roots stretching up over the ground in a way that creates a small recessed space against the tree. I move to the back side of the tree that faces away from the direction the guys will be coming from, but a flash of pink stops me in my tracks and I jump back instinctively.

"Get the fuck out of here," Kyla hisses.

I should turn and walk away, but I can't help rolling my eyes and retorting, "It's not like I knew you'd be here."

"I don't give a fuck. Find somewhere else."

Obviously. Except, this is right around where Grant is expecting me to be. How far can I go before it becomes a problem? My mind races, trying to figure out what to do. This is where Grant will look for me first. Fuck.

I don't have time to think, so I head deeper into the woods and hope that Grant is able to find me in time.

Managing to find another tree next to a massive fallen branch, I nestle into the spot where they meet so I'm covered on my back and side. I crouch, trying to make myself as small as possible, and I'm suddenly very grateful for the black fabric covering me head-to-toe. Even in the dark, Kyla's bright, shimmery dress caught my eye, but I'm practically invisible.

The minutes tick by, each one stretching longer than the last. I'm starting to feel uneasy, the anticipation eating at me. I try to shake the feeling off, focusing on listening for Grant's voice. There's a shout in the distance that makes my entire body tense, but it's immediately followed by laughter. Every sound feels magnified, every rustle of leaves or snap of a twig sending my mind spiraling into fear.

I let out a breath, shaking my head at myself for being so jumpy, until leaves crunch near me in what is undoubtedly a footstep. Then another. And another, each one getting closer and closer to me.

I risk a peek around the tree, and my blood freezes when I see Mason creeping toward me, his creepy ass mask hanging around his neck.

Panic rises in my chest. He saw me. I immediately turn to run, but I can still hardly see. I try anyway, only making it a few steps before he closes in on me and grabs my arm, his fingers digging into my bicep. I stumble, desperately trying to pull away from him, but he only tightens his grip. My skin crawls at the memory of the last time he touched me and panic bubbles up in my throat.

I thrash around, fighting back, but he easily overpowers me with his size. "Always playing hard to get." His lips are too close to my ear and his breath is hot on my neck. "You may have gotten away last time, but this time, you're mine."

No. No. I won't let this happen. I manage to jab my elbow into his stomach and he hisses with pain.

"Ouch, you little fucking bitch," he seethes. But his grip only tightens, restricting my movement more. Think, Sadie, think. I can barely form a coherent thought from the terror gripping me as he twists my arms behind my back and uses one of his own to force them into place while his other hand skims my torso.

"Stop! I quit! I'm done!" But even in the midst of my fear, I know saying that won't work. This isn't part of the challenge to him; it's revenge. I should know from last time that my protests will do nothing.

"You don't want to forfeit the challenge, do you?" His voice is sickly sweet, cajoling in a way that makes my skin crawl. "We all know you're desperate for that money," he sneers. "Just let me have you for tonight. One night with me and you get to walk away with all that money." He brushes a strand of hair from my face with his free arm as I twist to get free, and it makes me want to vomit.

"No. Fuck you. Let. Me. Go."

He chuckles in response. "I don't think I will."

"Sadie?" It's not Mason's voice this time. It's Grant's.

"Over here!" I yell, relief washing over me as he rushes over. Mason drops my arms and steps back, and I immediately move over to Grant's side. He rubs a reassuring hand on my back, but there's fury in his eyes as he watches Mason look around for an escape. He's in the same place I was hiding, cornered between the tree and the fallen branch.

Grant's hand drops from my back as he steps toward Mason. Mason may be big, but Grant is bigger, not to mention an athlete.

"And just what the fuck do you think your were doing with her?" Grant's voice is low and level, terrifyingly calm.

Mason, given the option to run, beg for mercy, or be a raging douchebag, chooses the latter option. "Please," he scoffs. "She needs some good dick to calm her down so she's not such a stuck-up bitch all the time."

Grant's fist connects with Mason's face before he even has time to react. Mason stumbles back, his hand reaching up to touch his bloodied nose, before lurching toward Grant. Grant easily dodges him and lands another punch, then another, and there's the sound of a sickening crunch before Mason collapses on the ground.

He's still moving, rolling to his side, but clearly incapacitated.

Grant turns to me, fire still burning in his eyes. "If I were you, I'd kick this piece of shit while he's down. Literally."

I don't think twice. I walk over to him and kick him in the ribs as hard as I can, the impact shooting through my leg. Then I do it again. And again. He's moaning and rolling around on the ground, attempting to cover himself with his arms.

I step back. I should probably be concerned by the fact that I don't feel any remorse from my violence. But when I look at him lying on the ground, I'm filled with disgust—not at myself, but at him. Who knows how many other women he's taken advantage of. That pathetic excuse of a man deserves a lot worse than a broken rib or two.

I turn silently and walk away, Grant by my side.

"Fuck. Thank you," I finally whisper, my voice shaking as Grant pulls me into him. The heat of his body is comforting as we walk back through the forest.

He tilts his head down to look at me. "Are you okay?" he asks, concern etched into his features.

"I'm fine," I manage, trying to steady my voice. "This isn't the first time something like that has happened with him. I was so scared I wouldn't be able to get away this time." Tears spill from my eyes, whether from relief or the adrenaline comedown, I'm not sure.

"What happened with him before?" Grant asks. "If you're comfortable telling me."

"He asked me on a date senior year but wanted to keep it quiet. I just assumed it was because I was the weird girl and he didn't want his friends knowing we were going out. Well, his parents were out of town, so we hung out and watched a movie at his house. He started getting touchy, I asked him to stop, and he didn't stop. I was trying not to freak out because I realized by that point that if I started to fight, he'd only fight back harder. I made the excuse of needing to go to the bathroom before things went any further, and then I snuck out the back door and ran all the way home."

"Fuck, I'm so sorry that happened."

"He's a terrible person," I say. "But thank you for saving me. Seriously."

He squeezes me against his side. "No problem. I've gotta protect my new partner in crime."

I can't help but smile at his words. Why do I like the sound of that so much?

"Okay, so I have to ask," he starts, his voice turning serious again. "With all of that having happened, is there anything specific that might trigger you if these challenges get more sexual? I don't know exactly what else is going to happen tonight, but I do have an idea, and I think there's a good chance of things getting more intense sexually."

I think for a moment before answering, "No, I don't think so. As long as it's not with him, I'll be okay."

"And what about other people getting involved?"

"Hmmm. I think I'll be okay as long as one of us knows them."

He's quiet for a moment before simply saying, "Okay."

I'm almost certain he knows something I don't.

As we emerge from the woods, the distant sound of the party grows louder, the music and cheers a familiar, grounding presence. Grant picks me up and carries me over the finish line, both of us laughing and giddy from relief. There are still fifteen minutes left on the timer.

Cam checks off our names on his clipboard, and we both sink into a couple empty chairs on the porch to wait for the rest of the couples to return. Two are already back, which means three others are still out there.

The crowd of partygoers has also lessened significantly in the time I've been gone.

"What time is it?" I ask Grant.

"Past 2, I think."

Damn, no wonder there are fewer people. It also makes sense that most of the thrill-seekers would leave, not wanting to sit here and wait an hour for everyone to return. Though there are likely quite a few who have gone back into the house for the time being. It's fucking cold out here.

But still, Grant and I sit side-by-side, staring out toward the dark woods and waiting for the competition to return. I can only hope for less competition in whatever messed-up challenge comes next.

CHAPTER SIX

I DRINK SOME water—which is the last thing I expected to be drinking at a Halloween party—as Grant and I wait out the last fifteen minutes of the challenge. One couple returns a few minutes after us, and I'm surprised to see Kyla returning before the timer runs out, only she's with one of the men who had been partnered up with someone else. I wonder how that happened.

She gives me a scathing look as she walks up onto the porch, but I simply smile back at her, knowing I left her boy toy half-conscious in the dirt. Really, I'm doing her a favor.

The timer counts down, everyone having returned aside from Mason and whoever was with Kyla's new partner previously. A.J. and Jimmy eagerly bring the fireworks to the middle of the yard and light them, running back right before they fly into the air and explode in a shower of sparks with a deafening bang!

Cam looks down at his clipboard, noting that one of the other girls is missing as well as Mason. "Alright, y'all, we're going to send a couple people out with flashlights if the last two participants haven't come back in five minutes or so. Try to mentally prepare yourselves for the rest of the night, because things have been fairly tame up to this point, and shit's about to get real." He laughs to himself, and for the first time tonight, his happy-go-lucky attitude isn't entertaining—it's concerning. He genuinely seems to be telling what he believes to be the truth, so if things have been "tame," as he said, I can't help but feel dread crawling down my spine at the idea of what he might consider to be the more serious challenges.

People drift out onto the porch again, ready for whatever challenge Cam is about to throw at us next. Quite a few are stumbling, having had the last hour to drink without other entertainment.

The air is tense, the artificial light from the porch lights and Halloween string lights casting an unsettling glow over the scene before us. A.J. and Jimmy are setting up a small fold-out table away from the crowd but are close enough that I can kind of make out what they're doing. I squint, trying to discern what tiny items their fingers are arranging.

"Okay, this next challenge will be done one-by-one. Again, the ladies are the stars of the show, so they'll be the only ones participating this round." I shift on my feet, unsettled by the idea of doing something without Grant, who has weirdly become a beacon of safety for me in the matter of the past few hours.

"The table that the guys set up over there has ten pills on it. You each have a choice to make. Pick one, take it, and hope it was the right choice. Some are

60

harmless, and some might make things . . . interesting for the rest of your night."

The girl to the left of me speaks up, a nervous tremor in her soft voice. "What if we're on medications that could interact with whatever we take?" she asks.

Cam simply shrugs. "Then choose wisely. Or drop out."

She hesitates, her eyes darting from the table with the pills to her partner. It's a gamble either way, but I can see her decision form as her face falls and she throws up her hands. "I guess I'm out." Disappointment laces her words, but I can't blame her. We've all done so much to get to this point, so dropping out now must be devastating. She leaves, her partner in tow, and the tension ratchets up another notch as the number of couples dwindles to four.

"Anyone else?" Cam looks between the four of us, but none of us make a sound. "Great!" He smiles as if this is the most normal situation ever and not an incredibly risky and fucked up game.

"I have everyone's names written on a piece of paper here in this bowl. Can I get someone from the audience to draw them?"

People raise their hands and shout out, and Cam picks someone from the crowd. The wicked gleam in Cam's eye is stronger than before, almost sinister now. He's enjoying this way too much.

"Lily," Cam reads the first paper, "is the one who just left, so she's out." He tosses the paper over his shoulder. They draw another paper. "Kyla!"

Kyla's smug expression as she walks past me makes me want to smack it right off her face. I wish I was shocked that she's still holding on to high school drama, but I'm really not. Some people need that self-imposed conflict to feel superior, but she's always been one of those people and probably always will be.

She walks up to the table and surveys the pills before plucking one up and popping it in her mouth, swallowing it down with a cup of water before sticking her tongue out to show Cam and A.J. her empty mouth. They make her lift her tongue as they inspect to make sure she actually swallowed the pill instead of hiding it in her mouth. Smart call on their part, even if this is incredibly fucked up.

Another paper is pulled from the bowl. "Sadie!"

Fuck, that's me. I walk up to the table and survey the nine pills laid out for taking. My mind kicks into gear, cataloging what I know, and I'm incredibly grateful in this moment that I'm going into the medical field. There's ibuprofen, which I recognize instantly, along with acetaminophen. Next to it, Xanax and what I'm pretty sure is Percocet. There are two capsules that look like herbal supplements, and one bright pink tablet in the shape of a smiley face that is undoubtedly ecstasy. Wow, they didn't skimp out, I think wryly. I can't tell exactly what the other two pills are, but I'm pretty sure one of them is another opioid and the other might be some sort of vitamin.

I pick up the ibuprofen, take the offered cup of water, and wash it down. After proving to the guys that I've swallowed it, I take my spot back at Grant's side.

"I'm really glad I paid attention in pharmacology," I whisper to him. "They've got some strong shit up there."

"What did you take?" he asks.

"Just ibuprofen."

I crane my neck but can't see which pills the other two pick. The last girl hesitates, reaching for one before pulling back and picking another. One wrong move could result in an altered mental state that could cost her a place in the competition. She takes the pill and walks back to her partner, her eyebrows drawn together in concern.

"Awesome! Time for a much-deserved break," Cam announces, clapping his hands together like we've just finished a particularly grueling workout. What a psycho. "You've got thirty minutes to do what you need to do. Go to the bathroom, get a drink, or run while you still can." Most of the spectators laugh, but those of us participating look around with growing concern.

At the same time, a bizarre mix of relief and anticipation mix in my gut as I let out a heavy sigh. One more challenge down and three couples left to beat. I can do this. The night has to be almost over, right?

"I'm gonna go to the bathroom," I tell Grant. He nods, and I head through the maze of people until I find the open door.

The bathroom is dim with only the essentials, but mostly clean. As I'm washing my hands, I catch my reflection in the mirror. This is usually the part in the movies where the character doesn't recognize themselves, where the moral dilemmas and

63

questionable choices morph their face into something filled with horror and regret. But all I see is me—eyes bright with adrenaline, hair wild from the wind, and makeup a little smudged but otherwise fine.

I try to fix my eyeliner, wiping at it with a finger until it looks marginally better, and run a hand over my hair in an attempt to tame it. Maybe I'm crazy for not feeling any sort of regret for what I've done tonight despite the humiliation and dangerous situations, but I don't. If it wasn't me doing it, someone else would probably be in my place. It's just one night, after all, and the risk has been worth the potential reward. At least so far.

Back in the living room, Cam is waiting with a beer in hand and a self-satisfied grin plastered on his face. "Ready for the next round?" He looks every bit the deranged ringmaster with his expression and his costume. I give him a thumbs up and walk past him, grabbing a beer of my own. I don't know what the rest of the night holds, but I'm betting I'll need the liquid courage.

When I find Grant, he's standing near the back door, his head bowed as he talks to Jimmy. When I clear my throat, he steps back quickly but gives me a smile. "Feeling okay?"

"Yeah, I'm good," I tell him.

He gives Jimmy a lingering look before they both nod and Jimmy walks away. "Great. Well in that case, I'll join you for a drink," he says.

"Cool. What was that all about?" I ask as we make our way toward the cooler.

Grant leans down to whisper, "I may have rigged a small part of the next challenge."

CHAPTER SEVEN

"Only three left," Cam says, as if stating the obvious somehow heightens the drama. He really has a flair for the dramatic. "Congratulations. You've made it this far."

The words hang in the air, and I can only wonder what comes next. My heart pounds against my ribcage. I look at the others, wondering if they feel the same mix of dread and determination. Kyla looks up just as my eyes pass over her, and she smirks, giving me a pointed stare before returning her attention to Cam.

I resist the urge to roll my eyes. I'm still not entirely sure what she has against me, but her bitchy attitude makes me want to win this game even more. A ton of money and seeing the defeat in her eyes? That would make this more than worth it.

"Wait!" Someone shouts when Cam starts to speak again. All heads turn in the direction of the voice.

Mason stands there, covered in dirt with a bruise already forming around his swollen eye. He must have come back at some point while we were taking our break. Either that or someone found him and brought him back.

"What? I already told you you're disqualified, Mason."

"That's not what I'm worried about," he replies. "I just came here to tell you that she—" he turns and points to me with an evil smile "—dropped out when we were in the woods. She literally said, 'Stop, I'm quit.'"

Every eye in the crowd drifts to me.

"Is this true?" Cam asks.

Yes, I think, but only because he tried to rape me. Still, I can't say that for fear of being kicked out of the competition. "Oh, honey," I say to Mason in my most condescending voice, "I think you hit your head too hard. You should probably lie down." Then, I turn to Cam. "He tried to grab me and I fought him off. My man here might have something to do with that black eye, though."

Grant chimes in, his voice even and casual. "It's true. He found her first, but I showed up when she was fighting with him. If she had told him she quit, then he would have had to let her go and moved on, right?" His eyes flick over to Mason then back to Cam. "He's just bitter because he got his ass kicked and disqualified."

"That's not true!" Mason protests.

Cam turns to face him. "So, you're telling me that she told you no but you kept touching her then?

Because your face will look a lot worse here in a few seconds if that's the case."

Mason realizes his mistake and, knowing he's caught in a trap, mumbles, "No. This is bullshit," before he stomps away.

"Anywayyyy," Cam resumes. "This is the second-to-last challenge of the night, so we're gonna make things interesting." As if they haven't been interesting this entire night. I can only wonder what his idea of 'making things interesting' is if it hasn't happened already.

As if on cue, his buddies A.J. and Jimmy make their way outside. A.J. hands Cam three long, thin pieces of rope while Jimmy carries a duffel bag to the table we had taken pills from earlier, which has since been cleared.

The sight of the ropes has my stomach flip-flopping. Three ropes makes it pretty easy to guess that there's one for each of us.

Cam points above our heads. "Not sure if you noticed earlier, but there are hooks in the roof. They're meant to hold swings or hammocks, so I think they'll hold each of you ladies just fine."

I swallow hard. I don't like where this is going.

"Now, you won't be completely suspended, but we're tying your arms up, and . . . well, I'll explain the rest after we get you all situated." He's again wearing that now all-too-familiar look of enjoyment at our discomfort.

Each of our partners heads over to Cam at his request, and Cam speaks to them all for a moment before handing each a long stretch of rope. The guys return to us a few seconds later, and each pair finds a hook to stand under.

"You okay with this?" Grant whispers to me after he manages to get the rope looped over the hook above me. It's clear that he's remembering the situation with Mason and wondering if I can handle being restrained, and likely touched by someone other than him.

"Yes, I'm okay," I whisper. Then, even quieter, "Is this what you rigged?"

"Arms up," he instructs before answering, "Yes. They're going to pull names of people who get to play with you. I paid off Jimmy to read the names of my friends, who agreed to help." As he speaks, he makes intricate loops with the rope around my wrists. Each tightening layer makes my breath quicken, though surprisingly more with anticipation than fear. I've had a little fun with bondage during the past, but never with more than one person and definitely not in front of a crowd.

Grant's fingers trail over the skin of my wrist, since that's really the only skin exposed on me right now, but my tight clothing and outstretched position leaves very little to the imagination. Even fully covered, I feel exposed and vulnerable as he takes a step back to survey his work.

"Pull on those as hard as you can," he instructs. I do, but the knots hold tight, and his lips quirk up at the edges as he watches me test the rope. Hmmm, looks like Grant may not be as much of a vanilla good guy as I thought . . . One thing's for sure—he definitely knows how to tie some good knots.

An image flashes through my mind of him hovering above me with me restrained to a bed, his hands teasing and caressing and—

Fuck, I need to stop thinking like this right now. Focus, Sadie. You've got a competition to win.

As soon as the other women are restrained, Cam places each of our buckets in front of us. All the money is still in them from the previous challenges, and I'm just close enough to the others to see that theirs aren't far off. It's impossible to tell who's in the lead until the money's counted.

The pressure is on.

After Cam inspects each of us to make sure the ropes are tight and secure, he resumes his place in front of the crowd. Everyone's expressions are ravenous now, ready for any sort of vile, fucked up thing Cam can think of.

The announcement of the challenge goes just how Grant told me it would—Cam explains that two names per couple will be pulled from a bucket where they had collected the names of eager participants earlier. When Cam gestures to the table, I look over, having forgotten all about A.J. and his duffel bag. The table is covered in all sorts of sexual implements, from vibrators to floggers to ball gags and more.

Oh.

I glance over at Kyla, who has the same self-satisfied look on her face that she's had all night, then I look over at the other girl to my left. Her face is blank—no excitement, no fear, nothing. Her partner is stroking her hair and whispering something in her ear.

More rules and explanations. "This will be the biggest tipping event for tonight, so make sure you have your cash ready," Cam tells the crowd.

God, I really need this. The idea that I might have gone through all of this tonight only for someone else to win the challenge—Kyla especially—sends a pang of fear through me. All this for nothing . . . No, it's not an option. I'm winning this. We're winning this.

"This challenge will last twenty minutes, so there's a lot of time for fun. Any questions?" Silence. "Then time to draw some names!"

They draw two names for Kyla first, and the two guys who are chosen eagerly make their way over to her. Their eyes are practically bugging out of their heads as they zero in on her tits.

Two names are called for the other girl, whose name is apparently Yasmin. I don't know if she's terrified or really just unbothered, because her expression is still unreadable.

Finally, it's my turn. Even though Grant told me he rigged it, I can't help but worry that Jimmy will go back on their deal. Mason's eyes pierce me from the back of the crowd, and my body goes rigid at the thought of his name being pulled. I'll deal with a lot of shit for this money, but I can't handle him touching me again. I'd lose it.

Fuck, please let the names called be Grant's friends. As Jimmy reaches into the bucket, my stomach is in knots. He reads off the names—Xavier and Emmett—and they step forward. They're smiling, but not in the cruel, hungry way the others were. Grant rubs gentle circles on the small of my back, letting me know I'm safe. I let out a slow breath, calming myself, but the sight of the bucket not far from my feet doesn't allow me to calm down entirely.

I have to win this. There's no other choice for me now, at least in my mind. If they're making this an all-or-nothing challenge, then I'm taking it all, no matter what the rest of the night may hold.

Grant is whispering to Xavier as we wait for Cam to start the timer, but I whisper his name just loud enough for him to look up.

"Grant!" It's quiet, but he hears the urgency in my voice and rushes over.

"Yeah? Are you okay?"

"I'm fine," I tell him, "but listen. I need to win this. As stupid as it sounds, the money is kind of a big deal for me."

"Okay . . ." His brow furrows as he waits for the rest of whatever I'm about to say.

"So, I don't know what you guys are whispering about over there, but we need to put on a show to fill that bucket. The more we entertain them, the more money we'll get."

"So, what are you saying?"

"I'm saying don't hold back. Any of you. I trust you, which might be crazy considering the circumstances, but it's true. And if you trust them, then so do I. Give these people what they want to see." I nod toward the remaining partygoers—probably down to about thirty—who look ready to pounce. "They want a show, and we're going to give it to them."

Grant grins. "If you're willing, then I'm absolutely in." I can tell he's plotting now, lustful thoughts flashing behind his eyes. I knew he'd probably think I was too afraid to go to extremes, but he needs to understand that, with the right man and a high level of trust, I'm willing to try just about anything. Mason may have made me paranoid about shitty, predatory men, but Grant has somehow managed to earn my trust and affection in the matter of one night.

For the first time tonight, I fully return his smile. "Let's do it."

CHAPTER EIGHT

A minute later, Cam sets the timer and announces the start of the challenge, the energy around us turning frenzied.

Xavier and Emmett step back as Grant steps in front of me and surveys me, his gaze consuming my outstretched body. At the beginning of the night I had pegged him as cute, flirty, and maybe even a little basic, but now as I look up at him, I realize I have vastly underestimated him. Everything about him right now screams dominance, from his predatory expression to the way he stands tall and confident. But what gets me most is the look in his eyes. In them, I can see that this isn't just a show for him—he wants to do this, whatever this ends up being.

In an instant, Grant wraps his arm around my waist and pulls my body against his, kissing me hard. His lips are soft but demanding. Somehow, it feels more intense and vulnerable than anything we've done so far tonight. My stomach swoops, and I'm breathless when he finally steps back.

"Ready?"

"Yes," I breathe.

He circles me, stopping behind me and resting his hands on my waist. When I feel his large body press against my back, I let my head roll back to rest on his chest and close my eyes, wanting to focus more on him than the group of people staring at me.

His hands trail up the front of my body until they reach my breasts. He squeezes them firmly and continues to knead them as he leans down to whisper in my ear.

"If you need any of us to stop what we're doing without risking forfeiting the competition, say my name instead of saying 'stop.' Understand?"

I nod. "Mhmm."

Our conversation is cut short by cries not far from where we stand. "Stop, stop, stop!"

Everyone freezes. I look over to see the other participant, Yasmin, shaking her head quickly and protesting. The two men whose names had been drawn step back immediately while her partner quickly works at the knots holding her wrists. Her eyes are barely open despite her apparent effort to keep them from closing.

Shit, she must have taken one of the more potent pills earlier. As soon as her hands are free, she drops into her partner's arms, clinging to him as he rubs his hand over her back to calm her down.

They head into the house, surrendering their money to Cam on the way in, and everyone's attention snaps back to us.

Only two of us left. It feels more real now than it has all night, so close I can taste it.

I turn my head to look at Kyla as the frenetic energy of the crowd bounces back almost immediately. All three of her guys seem to be trying to get their fill, their hands tugging at the neckline and hem of her tiny dress.

It's just the two of us now, and I know she has the advantage as the thin, pretty blonde, so the pressure is on to put on a show for these people and get as much money as we can.

Grant must be thinking the same thing, because he jumps into action. In an instant, he's put on a showy, cocky persona and faces the crowd. "What should I do with her?" He says as if pondering, but he speaks loudly enough that it's clear he's addressing the people watching.

"Take her clothes off!" someone shouts.

My stomach drops, not because I'm worried about being naked in front of these people—though that thought is still anxiety-inducing—but because I'm wearing a one-piece outfit that I can only slip out of through the top. With my hands tied above my head and presumably not allowed to be untied, there's not really a way to undress me. Disappointing the first person to make a suggestion isn't exactly a great way to start this challenge.

Grant doesn't seem to realize this yet, because he flashes a grin as he makes his way toward me. He reaches into his pocket as he takes the last step and pulls out a pocket knife. Well, fuck. I guess I was wrong.

He stands in front of me but takes a step sideways so that everyone has a clear view of what he's about to do. "Stay still," he commands, reaching up and pulling the fabric away from my neck before flicking open his knife in one hand and slicing all the way down to my bra. He makes a tsk sound before saying, "Well, this has to go too."

"Wait," I whisper. "Don't cut it. It's strapless; just unhook it in the back."

He slips the knife onto his waistband and reaches around to unhook my bra before tossing it on the ground behind me. I see him lift his chin at his friends to signal . . . well, something. I'm not sure what.

Grant pulls the knife from his waistband and continues the process of cutting down the center of my outfit, exposing more skin with every inch. My nipples are hard beneath the fabric, only barely concealed after losing my bra and having my bodysuit split open. He goes further and further until he's cut all the way down to the crotch of the outfit. I think he's about to put the knife away, but he doesn't. Instead, he twists it in his hand and begins tracing the tip over my bare skin.

"Does it scare you?" He asks, low enough for only me to hear.

"Does what scare me?"

"That I have you all tied up right here and can do anything I want to you because you want to win this so badly you'll refuse to give up."

My muscles tense. Fuck, he's got a point. Realistically I know that if I say "stop" I'll be safe, but he's right about me refusing to give up. I'm in this too far to quit now. He's likely just saying it to get a reaction out of me, but it's sure as hell working.

I want to twist and squirm away, but I can't. The rope is too tight, and I don't want to risk moving so much with the knife still on my skin. The only movement my body makes is my chest rising and falling with rapid breaths.

Grant smirks, knowing exactly what kind of reaction he's giving me. He drags the knife across my skin, lower and lower, switching between the flat side of the blade and the tip, which leaves thin pink scratches streaking over my torso.

The cold blade of the knife reaches my panties, and I hold my breath wondering what Grant's next move is. He twists the knife so that the flat side pushes against the front, putting pressure on my clit and making me terrified to move. He simply stares at me, a smile playing at his lips. He removes it a few seconds later, but it feels like much longer.

He slips the knife back into his pocket and grabs the fabric where it's split over my chest and pulls outwards, exposing my breasts and even more of my bare stomach. My nipples pebble in response to the wave of cold air washing over them, the rest of my skin breaking out in goosebumps.

People shout in excitement from the crowd, and heat rises to my cheeks. I risk another glance over at Kyla, who seems to be having a good time, but her body is obscured by the bodies of the three other men all trying to selfishly get their fill of her while they can.

I don't realize that Xavier and Emmett had stepped away until they're walking in front of me with items in their hands that they must have snagged from the table. Xavier hands Grant whatever he's concealing in his fists, but Emmett saunters up to me with a flogger in his hand.

"Ready?" he asks. There's a glint in his eyes that tells me he's about to enjoy this.

I nod.

He flicks the tails of the flogger over his palm a few times to test the sensation before he reaches out to trail it over my body.

The ends of the flogger brush lightly over my skin, teasing me. Emmett draws it across my breasts and down over my stomach. My nipples harden in anticipation as he moves lower and strikes the back of my thigh gently. I let out a soft gasp at the sensation, more from surprise than anything else.

He increases the intensity gradually, flicking the tails against me with more force. Each strike makes me flinch with the slight sting as he switches up the location from my thighs to my ass. Despite the pain— or because of it—I ache for more, twisting and pulling against the ropes. Emmett seems to sense my enjoyment and desire for more, bringing the flogger down harder.

I moan and let my head fall back as he takes a couple steps to stand directly in front of me. He eases up slightly on the intensity but brings the flogger down on my chest.

My breathing grows ragged as the strikes land on my tits, sharp and stinging. It hurts, but it feels so damn good.

Just when I think I can't take anymore, he pauses, looking over at Grant. My skin tingles and burns, and I fucking love it.

Emmett steps back and Grant steps forward. When I finally see what he's holding in his hands, my eye grow wide. Nipple clamps.

When he sees my reaction, he simply raises his eyebrows in amusement. He's enjoying my discomfort entirely too much. So why does that turn me on even more?

He clips on one side to my already hard nipple, then the other, and I inhale sharply. Fuck, that hurts. But it only takes a moment for the sharp twinge of pain to transform into a deep, dull ache.

Grant leans in to speak to me without anyone else hearing. "I bet you're already wet for me, aren't you?"

The sound that comes out of my mouth is something between a whine and a moan, but he takes it as all the approval he needs.

"I'll take care of that later, but first I'm going to keep playing with you until you're begging me to get you off." It sounds more like a threat than a promise.

He steps back and gently tugs at the chain hanging between the clamps, making me cry out again and pull against the ropes.

Emmett's strikes with the flogger begin again, harder and faster than before. I cry out, overwhelmed by the mix of pleasure and pain. I'm vaguely aware of people stepping forward and dropping money into our bucket, but I'm so overloaded with sensation that I can't actively pay attention to anything. And I definitely can't get cocky, because I haven't been paying attention to what Kyla's getting either.

Emmett continues his relentless pace with the flogger, every once in a while catching the small chain between the clamps, pulling at my already sensitive nipples. Each moan that slips from my lips seems to earn a reaction from the crowd, so I don't hold back.

But pretty soon, Kyla has realized what's happening and joins in on the fun. The sounds coming from her can only be described as 'overdramatic porn star.' She's clearly faking it and subscribing to the notion that louder equals better.

I glance in her direction and see a couple people dropping money into her bucket, but despite the fact that her dress is now only covering her stomach while leaving everything else exposed, the men are still obscuring the audience's view of her body as they grope at her.

Grant's voice drags me back to my own reality. "What should we do with her next?" he wonders aloud to the spectators.

"Make her cum!" someone shouts.

"Hmm, should I?" He looks back at me with raised eyebrows—he's still putting on a show, wearing that same cocky look, but I know he's actually checking in with me—and I nod almost imperceptibly.

I still feel the urge to hide my face from the expectant onlookers, embarrassed by my exposed state, but I know it's about to get much worse. Grant steps over to Xavier and Emmett, telling them something in hushed tones to which they nod in agreement. He walks over to the table and ponders over the wide array of toys and implements before picking something out, though he hides it behind his back before I can see what it is.

Heat radiates from his body as his body presses against my back. His voice is a low growl. "As fucked up as this situation is, I can't wait to see what you look like when you come. Though I'm selfish enough to wish I was the only one watching."

My thighs clench together in response, not only to his words but the dark tone lacing them. And he sounds like he means every bit of what he's saying.

Grant steps away, but the heat of his body is quickly replaced by another. What the—?

Before I can think about what's happening, I'm being lifted from behind on either side. Emmett holds one leg while Xavier has the other, and the cheers of the crowd grow louder. I grasp onto the rope above my head even though it doesn't really do anything besides give me a sense of stability. The men on my sides have got it under control. I lean back slightly, my shoulders pushing against each of their chests, as Grant reaches me in two slow, measured steps.

My stomach flips at the look in his eyes and the echo of his words still in my head. I can't wait to see what you look like when you come.

He reaches out and slides a finger over the top of my panties and smirks. This time, he speaks loudly enough so people might be able to hear. "Already so wet. I bet you secretly love being watched by all of these people while I show them what a dirty little slut you actually are."

My chest rises and falls with quick breaths.

"That's what I thought," he taunts when I have no reply. "Such an obedient little kitty."

I narrow my eyes at him but say nothing.

When he reveals the vibrator he's hidden behind his back, my jaw falls open. Oh, fuck.

I'm now hyper-aware of every eye on me as Grant clicks the button to the highest setting. Our gazes are magnetized to each other's—there's a glint in his eyes that stirs something deep within me.

When he touches the vibrator to my clit, my body reacts instantly. I try to squirm away and close my legs, but I can't. Emmett and Xavier have a tight hold on me, keeping my legs spread out and my body facing Grant and the crowd behind him. The crowd is smaller than it has been all night, but I feel more exposed than ever. It sends a mix of discomfort and excitement swirling through me.

Grant moves to the side slightly to give the crowd a better view as he rubs the vibrator along my slit, and I tune out the lewd comments being thrown my way.

The tension inside me builds higher and higher like a thread about to snap, and I know I'm getting close. "Fuck," I whimper.

"That's right, baby girl. Let me hear it," Grant coaxes.

"Two minutes!" Cam shouts.

Emmett reaches around and tweaks a nipple, rolling it between his fingers while Grant holds the vibrator unforgivingly against my clit.

I throw my head back, close my eyes, and surrender to the feeling. My orgasm hits hard and fast, and I cry out as it rolls through me. I'm vaguely aware of whistles and shouts of approval, but I can't focus on anything but the waves of pleasure washing over me again and again. The men's hold on me tightens, their fingers digging into my thighs and ass as my hips buck against the toy.

But as the orgasm fades, Grant doesn't let up. I'm panting, desperately trying to pull away from the now overwhelming sensation, but it's impossible. I whimper as I squirm in Xavier and Emmett's arms, unable to get away. My clit is throbbing and sensitive, and Grant simply chuckles at the look of pure desperation on my face.

"Three, two, one!" Cam calls out, and Grant pulls the toy away from me before clicking it off.

Emmett and Xavier gently set me down, and my vision seems to sway. Deep breaths, I remind myself as Grant works at the knots around my wrists. When he finally unties them, I drop my arms and rub them in an attempt to get some feeling back into them.

In my post-orgasm haze, I suddenly feel entirely too exposed with my now-ruined costume. I manage to pull the fabric just enough to cover my nipples, but that's about it. My panties are soaked and exposed to the cold night air, and the line of skin up the center of my torso is impossible to cover.

Cam stands there patiently, waiting for the noise from the audience to die down. Once it's mostly quiet, he speaks again.

"Only one more challenge for tonight, and possibly the most intense of all."

We wait on bated breath, the tension palpable. Almost there. I look down at my bucket then over at Kyla's, but the money is too close to tell. If this is the last challenge, I need to make it count. I'm winning this fucking thing.

CHAPTER NINE

AS IF ON cue, Jimmy walks out the back door and silently stands next to Cam, clearly having something to do with this challenge.

There's a glint in Cam's eyes as he says one word. "Tattoos!"

A lump forms in my throat. This can't be good.

He clears his throat to elaborate. "For the record, I'll have you know that I wanted this challenge to be branding instead of tattoos, but the guys told me it would be too problematic." He rolls his eyes, as if it's totally reasonable to be annoyed about people saying that burning something onto another human's skin is too extreme.

Thank god for small favors, I guess. A tattoo will last longer but hurt a hell of a lot less.

"Anyway, the ladies, as always, are the center of attention for the challenge. Their partners will be choosing one other person to do the tattoo, and whoever does it will get thirty minutes to create, well, whatever they want." The flash of teeth he shows isn't quite a smile.

"The rules for this challenge are that the tattoo must be at least two inches by two inches, the woman being tattooed is not allowed to see the tattoo until it is done, and she can't give any input or feedback on the tattoo design but is allowed to choose the location on her body."

My eyes are practically bugging out of my head as I look over at Grant. He shakes his head at me and gives me a small but reassuring smile.

"Nobody gets eliminated here, so if both of you choose to go through with it, then the winner will be determined by the money."

When I look over at Kyla, her eyes are flitting between Cam and her partner, clearly nervous about whatever might happen. But when she sees me looking at her, she straightens her shoulders before nodding at Cam. I do the same.

"Looks like we're on, then! Men, choose the person you want to tattoo your partner." Grant immediately chooses Xavier while Kyla's partner picks one of his friends—I still don't know either of their names.

The chosen tattooers head over to Jimmy, who apparently does tattoos pretty frequently, and he gives them a spiel on safety and keeping things clean, which is kind of hilarious to me given the circumstances. Better than them using dirty equipment, at least. We're instructed to go inside, and Kyla and I take seats on opposite sides of the room where there are small tables already set up with equipment.

We wait, watching the spectators filter in with drinks in hand and excitement lacing the conversations. Finally, the guys all walk back inside, and I hope whatever tattoo Grant and Xavier decided on is reasonable, and also that Xavier is a decent artist. Even with good art skills, I know tattoos are significantly more difficult to do.

"You better not tattoo any stupid shit," Kyla warns, "or I swear to god I'm going to make your life a living hell." Well, that's one way to not get someone on your good side. Her partner placates her, only to give his buddy a subtle fist bump and a grin behind her back.

She decides to get the tattoo on her ass, clearly not trusting them to tattoo anywhere it might be visible. I pick the side of my upper thigh. Grant cuts the fabric of my costume even more to expose my thigh without me needing to strip off the outfit entirely.

Once Cam comes in with his timer and we situate ourselves into position, with me lying on my side in a recliner and Kyla face-down on the couch.

"Everyone ready?" We give Cam a thumbs up. "Go!"

The buzzing of tattoo guns fills the room, but I can't watch. Grant kneels next to the recliner to face me.

"Have you ever had a tattoo before?"

I shake my head. "No. I want one but haven't been able to afford a good artist yet."

"Okay. It's basically going to feel a lot like a bunch of constant cat scratches, but from what I've gathered tonight, you're pretty good with pain."

I can't help but return his smile at that. "You're not wrong."

"Ready?" I hear Xavier ask.

"Yep!"

The needle bites into my skin and I immediately clench my teeth. It's not terrible, but it certainly doesn't feel good.

Grant pulls my hand into his. "Keep breathing and squeeze my hand if you need to. It'll be over before you know it."

"Okay," I breathe, taking up his offer to squeeze his hand. After a few minutes, I'm more used to the pain but still focusing on remembering to breathe. I notice Jimmy in the periphery, hovering between the two clusters of people to make sure the tattooers are following directions.

"You're doing so well," Grant encourages, and his praise ignites something inside me. His face is so close to mine, and I realize that despite all we've done tonight, we haven't kissed. And in this moment I want nothing more than for him to kiss me.

My head feels light, likely from my lack of sleep coupled with lust and the adrenaline from the pain of the tattoo. All of those combined have my mind feeling weirdly euphoric, as if I'm high even when I know I'm completely sober. Regardless of all of that, or maybe because of it, I want him to kiss me and touch me and give me all of his attention.

"Two more minutes!" Cam shouts some time later. I can't see Kyla from the position I'm in, but I can hear people making vague comments and laughing about her tattoo, and I can only imagine what her guys came up with. I silently hope that mine turns out okay and isn't something stupid, though I highly doubt Grant would have his friend tattoo something dumb on me.

"Time's up!" Cam calls out a couple minutes later. The tattoo guns are switched off and Xavier flashes me a smile as I stand.

"Hope you like it."

I twist my body slightly to peek down at my thigh.

"Oh my god, this is so cute!" It's a Halloween-themed line tattoo, with a small jack-o-lantern in the foreground on the bottom left side. The main part of the tattoo, though, is a ghost figure with cat ears, a tail, and whiskers. It's adorable.

Xavier grins at that, clearly proud of his work. "It's a little shaky, but I did the best I could."

"Seriously, I love it," I tell him. Then, looking at Grant, I say, "I'm assuming this was all your idea."

His lips twitch in a smile. "Yes. Figured you'd want something that fits you, but I also wanted it to be a reminder of tonight."

"Why? So I think about you every time I look down at my thigh?"

He flashes me a teasing smile at that. "Maybe. Though I'd like you to think of me in other ways too."

"What's that supposed to mean?"

"That I'd like to see you again after tonight. That is, if you still want to see me after all the debauchery we've gotten up to tonight."

"I'd like that," I say. "At least I already know you're at least as fucked up as I am, so we could at least go out on a real date without it getting weird. Or, at least not as weird as tonight." To be fair, Cam may be fucked up for thinking of all these challenges, but we're just as fucked up, if not more, for participating in them willingly.

"I'm holding you to that," he jokes.

Our conversation is interrupted by the commotion as Kyla keeps asking what her tattoo is, but nobody will tell her. She must have some sort of idea from all the laughter. I manage to catch sight of it right as she pulls her dress down over it. Oh, fuck, she's going to be pissed.

I'm not sure if it's because she's been a bitch to them or simply because they're guys in their mid-twenties, but regardless of reason, they've drawn a crude outline of a dick on her ass cheek, complete with hairy balls and droplets of cum erupting from the top. Yikes.

Grant and I immediately lock eyes and burst out laughing. I almost feel bad. Almost.

We congregate back out on the porch where Cam is postured to make another announcement.

"Now is the moment of truth," he says in a low, dramatic voice. "Time to count the money."

Time seems to move in slow motion as I stare at Jimmy, who counts the bills, then at A.J., who recounts them to confirm the number. My legs feel weak, as if they might collapse under me at any second. When they finish counting mine, they each individually tell Cam a number that he writes on his clipboard. No announcements this time—at least, not until all the money is counted. I'm sure Cam wants the opportunity to make it a big, theatrical reveal.

My pulse pounds in my ears as I watch them count Kyla's money. With every bill flicking through their hands, the knot in my stomach tightens. What if she wins? If I leave here tonight with no money and all these embarrassing memories, not to mention the permanent tattoo on my thigh, I'm going to be overwhelmed with regret. Even now, the sinking feeling is starting and I don't even know if I've won or lost.

Jimmy and A.J. repeat the counting process for Kyla and report their numbers to Cam, who writes it down and glances up at me and then at Kyla with an expression I can't quite place. He walks over and collects our money buckets without a word.

"Ladies and gentlemen," he starts. The crowd, which has diminished even more over the past half hour, goes quiet. "I'd like to announce the winner for this year's challenge."

Come on, get on with it. I shift on my feet, unable to stand still. Please let it be me.

"Winning by one-hundred and seven dollars, congratulations to . . . Sadie!"

Holy shit. Seriously? My jaw hangs open and I immediately look up at Grant.

"You did it!" He beams at me and grabs my shoulders. "You won!"

I shake my head in disbelief. "Holy shit," I breathe before correcting him. "We won."

"Let's be real, you did all the hard work." He's still grinning and pulls me into a tight hug. I hear Kyla bitching about this being "total bullshit," but I don't even care. She can hate me for the rest of her life if she wants to.

Grant leads me in my stupor over to Cam, who is slipping the rest of the money into the manila envelope.

"Congratulations," Cam says.

"Th-thank you. I still can't believe I won."

"Well, you put on a real good show tonight." He winks.

I laugh nervously. "Thanks." I take the envelope from his outstretched hand a second later. "I gotta ask," I say before we walk away. "Why do you do this? Hosting this challenge and everything?"

He simply shrugs. "It's fun. Not everything needs to have some greater purpose. Sometimes I just wanna do fucked up shit for the sake of debauchery."

Grant chuckles. "Told ya," he says under his breath.

CHAPTER TEN

We're turning to walk away from Cam when Grant says, "Hey, bro, I'm gonna steal a shirt from the spare room if that's cool."

"Yeah, sure, no problem."

Grant gets pulled aside by the guy he swapped shirts with earlier so they can switch back, and he drapes his leather jacket over my shoulders before wrapping his arm around me and leading me inside.

My mind is still reeling from the events of the past hour, and despite the exhaustion weighing down on me, my body buzzes with a renewed sense of exhilaration. We won. It's over. It still doesn't feel real, like some sort of crazy dream that I'll be waking up from at any second, but the stinging sensation on my thigh is proof enough that this is reality. My sleep-deprived brain is giddy with excitement, the adrenaline still rushing through me. There's no doubt that I'm going to crash hard later.

I walk ahead of Grant up the stairs, and he leads the way to a closed door once we get to the top. But as soon as I shut the door behind me with a soft click, Grant is pushing me up against the wall.

"What are you doing?" I gasp.

"You've been driving me crazy all fucking night," he murmurs, his voice dangerously calm. His fingertips trail up the skin of my torso where the fabric's been cut, making me shiver. We're alone now for the first time tonight, and somehow that makes me even more nervous than being watched by all those people did. It's more intimate, and we can't hide under the guise of this being for show anymore.

"I—I could say the same for you," I manage to stutter out.

"Hmm, is that so?" He lifts my chin with a finger so I'm staring directly up at him.

I nod, unable to form words.

But instead of kissing me or touching me more, he pulls away. My brow furrows in confusion as I watch him walk to one end of the room and pull something from his pocket before the soft glow of candle light illuminates his silhouette. He repeats the process two more times, leaving one candle on the top of the dresser and another on the bedside table.

"Setting the mood?" I tease.

He smirks. "Something like that." He slips the lighter back in his pocket and takes slow, deliberate steps toward me, and my core tightens in response. He stops only inches away, his body trapping me against the wall as I wait for what comes next.

Grant pulls his jacket off me and tosses it to the side then lifts his hands to caress my shoulders before slipping them under the fabric of my outfit and pulling it down my arms, exposing my naked chest. I lift my arms to pull them out from the sleeves and let them fall to my sides. Grant's gaze consumes me as he slowly continues to undress me, slipping the skintight fabric down my legs along with my panties. I use his shoulders to steady myself as I step out of the rest of my clothing.

I feel small as he stands back up, towering over me and taking in my naked body. I resist the urge to cross my arms over myself. If I've been able to handle everything else that's happened tonight, I can surely handle this, even if it feels ten times more vulnerable.

His arm slips around my waist and pulls me to his body. "Come here," he commands. "I need you."

Heat courses through my veins as he takes a few slow steps backward until we reach the bed. He falls back, pulling me on top of him so I'm straddling his lap. Everything from tonight comes rushing back— feeling him get hard while I gave him a lap dance, sucking him off and hearing his low groans as he came in my mouth, standing there tied up as he forced me to come.

I press my legs together, needing any sort of friction, and can already feel my wetness coating my inner thighs.

Grant reaches up, his hands roaming over my body and tracing each curve. I close my eyes and savor the feeling. When he reaches up and brushes his thumbs across my nipples, I let out a soft moan, the action sending a jolt of electricity straight to my core. I roll my hips, grinding on him, desperate for any kind of friction. This seems to flip a switch in him, because he immediately rolls over, flipping me onto the bed while he leans overtop of me, caging me in with his arms.

"So fucking beautiful," he appraises. He leans down, kissing me with such desperation that it steals my breath away. His tongue pushes past my lips, and I moan into the kiss, arching my back to press my body against his. This kiss is everything I've needed tonight, and in this moment I don't think I could ever get enough. It's filled with a desperate, primal need, and when he finally pulls back, I'm breathing hard and desperate for more. He dips his head to plant kisses along my jaw and down my neck, his teeth grazing the sensitive skin, and I tilt my head back to give him better access as I lose myself entirely in him.

Grant's eyes stay glued on me as he steps back just enough to unbutton his jeans, letting them drop to the floor to reveal his thick, hard cock. He stands there stroking himself while I lie there bared to him remembering the noises he made when his cock was in my mouth a few hours ago. Heat burns in my core as I shamelessly watch him stroke himself. The dark intensity in his eyes seems to pin me in place.

He reaches forward to trail his hand over my skin, his touch igniting sparks as he moves lower and lower. With a low hum of approval, he dips his finger between my legs and slips one inside me before adding another and pushing his thumb down on my clit. My body trembles at his touch, my hips lifting in response to his fingers, desperate for more—for everything he can give me.

Instead of continuing, he removes his fingers and takes a slow step toward me, his eyes darkening with desire as he shifts slightly, lining himself up with my entrance. Every muscle in my body tightens in anticipation. Looking up at him, I once again think about how his demeanor has shifted as the night has gone on. The man I'm currently looking at—so dominant and serious—is a far cry from the casually flirty and joking personality I met earlier. And I have to say, while the other side of him was fun, this side is downright filthy and hot as fuck.

Grant's gaze is heavy with lust as he hovers above me, his strong arms on either side of my head. I can feel the heat radiating off his body, and it makes me want to be entirely consumed by him. "Fuck, Sadie," he growls, his voice low and rough. "You have no idea what you do to me."

He moves his hands to grip my thighs as he pushes inside me, slow and steady, his fingers digging into my skin as he forces my legs to wrap around his waist and holds me in place. My pussy is throbbing, desperate for him to take me and use my body until I can't think straight. Grant settles between my legs, the thick head of his cock nudging at my entrance. I'm already so wet for him, my pussy throbbing as teases me, rubbing his tip up and down my slit.

Without another word, he thrusts into me with a force that steals my breath away, burying himself to the hilt. I cry out in response and grip the blanket at my side, overwhelmed by the feeling of him filling me so completely. He pulls out slowly before pushing back into me until he's at a quick, steady pace.

"Tell me what you need," Grant rasps as he pounds into me relentlessly, each thrust hitting that spot deep within me and sending waves of pleasure through my body.

I can hardly form a coherent thought, let alone a sentence. "You. More." I breathe.

He pulls out of me and pushes me across the bed so that my legs aren't hanging off anymore before climbing onto the bed and straddling me. He doesn't move to push back inside me, though. Instead, he reaches over to the bedside table and gingerly lifts one of the candles he's lit.

My eyes widen when I realize what he's about to do.

"Ever done this before?" he teases.

"No."

He cocks an eyebrow and gives me a mischievous smile. "You'll love it."

I sure hope he's right.

It feels silly to be nervous about trying something new like this considering all the filthy things I've done tonight, but I am. Before, I could excuse my actions as being for show, but now it's just the two of us with no one to impress and only our own motives to consider.

I watch as he slowly tilts the candle, the scene seeming to happen in slow motion. The first drop of melted wax hits my collarbone and I gasp, the sensation making my body erupt in goosebumps. It burns for only a fraction of a second before cooling and hardening on my skin. He repeats the action, then again, each drop making me flinch as I watch it fall across my torso.

My skin prickles, still sensitive from the flogger earlier, so the sensation is even more intense than it likely would be otherwise. Grant drizzles more wax across my chest, tracing the curves of my breasts, and I arch my back involuntarily, craving more of the pleasure and pain.

"How does that feel?" His voice is low and husky as he intently watches my expression.

"So good," I whine, barely recognizing my own voice.

"You're very responsive," Grant murmurs, his eyes dark with lust as he watches the wax pool on my skin. "I fucking love it."

He continues dribbling the hot wax lower over my stomach and hips. Everywhere it touches, my nerve endings spark to life. I'm panting now, my chest heaving as I struggle to catch my breath.

"You're so beautiful like this," Grant breathes. "All flushed and needy and dripping wet for me, decorated like my own pretty little painting."

I look down at myself and admire the contrast of the blood red wax on my pale skin. He's right; it does look pretty. Not to mention the idea of him marking me, even if in this temporary way, sends a pleasant chill through me. Then I remember the tattoo and realize he has marked me, even if he technically wasn't the one to do the tattoo. It's his in every way that matters, so every time I see it, I'll think of this night with him.

Why does that thought turn me on so much?

As if reading my thoughts, Grant sets the candle back on the side table and nudges my legs apart with his knee. "I need you," he says, more of a command than a request but one that I'll happily comply with.

He immediately thrusts into me, harder this time than the first, and I cry out in response. I grip his shoulders and rake my nails down his back as he fills me again and again.

The room is filled with the sound of skin smacking against skin and our moans, the thumping bass resounding from the party downstairs muted but still buzzing through the air.

Grant fucks me hard and fast, his movements almost animalistic. All I can focus on is his hot skin pressed against my own, his heavy body pinning me down, and his relentless thrusts building the tension in my core, winding me tighter and tighter.

My inner muscles clench around him at his punishing pace and my breathing grows shallow. But he doesn't slow down or stop. He continues to slam into me with a primal urgency that sets fire to every nerve in my body.

His fingers dig into my hips as he drives into me harder and harder. My own moans and whimpers become background noise as I'm consumed by the overwhelming sensations coursing through me.

"That's right. Come for me, Sadie," Grant demands. "Let me feel you come apart on my cock."

His words shoot straight to my core. Seconds later, I finally hit that peak of ecstasy, and it crashes over me like a tidal wave, leaving me trembling and gasping for air.

Every nerve ending seems to be on fire as he fucks me through my orgasm, my muscles clenching around him. With a low groan, he finds his release inside of me, his cock pulsing as he spills into me. I feel him shudder as he collapses on top of me. We lie there, both of us struggling to catch our breath as we come down from the high.

I don't know how much time passes, but when my eyes start drooping, I know I need to get up or I'll be sleeping here whether I want to or not.

I stand and stretch, still completely naked.

"I believe I was promised a shirt?" I say to Grant, who's splayed out on the bed in all his glory. Damn, he looks good.

"I suppose you'll have to be clothed to go downstairs," he muses, his eyes raking over my body. He sifts through the closet before tossing me a shirt and manages to find a pair of jeans in the dresser that mostly fit. "Hope he doesn't mind losing these," he chuckles.

I pull on the clothes, grab our envelope of money, and look at Grant, who's also now dressed. "Wanna split this now away from prying eyes?"

He shakes his head. "No. It's all yours."

"Absolutely not. I dragged you into this whole thing. The least I can do is split the money with you."

When I flip open the top of the envelope, he puts his hand over it. "Seriously, Sadie. You told me earlier how much you need it, and honestly, I really don't. Plus, you did all of the hard work tonight."

"Wow. Well . . . thank you," I manage to say. "This will really make a difference for me. Are you sure?"

He smiles, that charm from earlier tonight back in full swing. "I'm completely sure. However, I do have one request."

"What's that?"

"Go on a real date with me. I know usually the first date comes before the kinky sex and not after, but you don't strike me as a girl who likes to follow the rules anyway." He winks, and butterflies swarm my stomach.

I return his smile. "Deal. But for now, let's get out of here."

CHAPTER ELEVEN

I quickly realize I've left my phone in Brooklyn's car and have no way to get ahold of her. To make it worse, she has no idea that it's in the glove box and has probably texted me multiple times tonight to check in.

"Can I use your phone?" I ask Grant.

"Sure." He unlocks his phone and hands it over, and I type in Brooklyn's number and shoot off a quick text letting her know I'm okay. I at least know where she hides her spare key, so I can get into the house fine.

"Everything okay?" Grant asks, his eyebrows lifting in concern.

"Yeah, it's just that Brooklyn was my ride here and I left my phone in her car. And she sleeps like the dead, so she probably won't see my text for another five hours."

"I can give you a ride if that works for you."

"That would be great, actually."

We make our way downstairs, our steps seeming to echo in the house now that the music has ceased. The house feels eerily quiet and empty now with only a few stragglers left, most of them passed out on couches or finishing their drinks with droopy eyelids as they attempt to keep up their conversations. Cam gives us a cheerful wave as we make our way out the door.

We step out of the house, and the chill in the early morning air is sobering. It's still pitch dark outside aside from the cheap Halloween lights flickering on the porch and the specks of stars dotting the sky.

I follow Grant down the gravel road to his car, the night's events swirling in my head like a hazy dream, still too surreal to fully believe. The adrenaline that had coursed through my veins during the challenge is now dissipating, leaving behind a strange mix of shame and exhilaration. I glance at the time—4:15 a.m.

He opens the passenger door for me, a gesture that feels almost out of place after the debauchery of the party. As I slide into the seat, I catch a glimpse of myself in the rearview mirror. My hair's a mess, makeup smeared, and I definitely don't look like someone who's ready for anything other than bed. Not to mention the oversized clothes I snagged from Cam's guest room.

Grant slides into the driver's seat and turns to face me. "I have a proposition."

"What would that be?"

"Would you maybe want to pregame our real date with some breakfast?"

I laugh. "Actually, food sounds fucking phenomenal right now."

He gives me that easy, confident smile, and for the first time tonight, I relax. "Well, Waffle House may not be the pinnacle of a fancy date, but it's pretty much the only option we've got right now," he says. "Is that good with you?"

I can't help but laugh at the absurdity of it all. Waffle House at 4 a.m. after a Halloween party where I just did something I never thought I would? Yeah, why not. What's one more impulsive decision for the night? "Sure," I say. "Though I look like trash right now."

"It's Halloween at a Waffle House. They expect people to be drunk and messy. Besides, I can promise you, you'll probably still be the best-looking person there."

"Not sure if that's a compliment about my attractiveness level or a jab at the Waffle House clientele, but either way, I'll take it."

Grant chuckles as he pulls out of the driveway, the gravel crunching under the tires beneath us. The streets are deserted, bathed in the orange glow of streetlights. It's the kind of quiet that only comes in the dead of night, where the world feels like it's holding its breath just before it comes to life.

I lean back in the seat, my eyes heavy as the adrenaline finally begins to fade. The reality of what I did tonight starts to sink in, and with it, a strange sense of satisfaction. Sure, it was fucked up—way beyond anything I've ever done before—but there was something empowering about it too. Like I'd crossed a line I never knew existed, and now I'm standing on the other side a little braver.

"You okay?" Grant asks, glancing over at me.

"Yeah, just... processing, I guess," I say with a small smile. "Tonight was intense."

"Tell me about it," he agrees. "I knew things got crazy there, but I still didn't expect things to get that wild. But at least we survived."

"Barely," I laugh. I suppress a shudder as I think about Mason's antics, but I'm hopeful he learned his lesson.

We pull into the parking lot of the Waffle House, the neon sign flickering slightly and bathing the parking lot in yellow light. There are a few cars scattered around, the usual late-night crowd of truckers, night owls, and hungover or half-drunk people.

Grant parks the car and turns to me. "I don't know about you," he says, his expression suddenly serious, "but I'm ready for some goddamn hashbrowns."

I laugh and shake my head at him. "Then by all means, let's go."

Inside, the place is as dingy as I expected, but there's a comfort in its familiarity. The smell of greasy food hangs in the air, and the worn vinyl booths have seen better days. We find a booth near the back, away from the few other patrons.

A waitress comes over, looking half-asleep herself, and takes our order without much interest. We both order way too much food, starving after the late-night drinking and all the physical activity of the night.

"So," Grant says, leaning back in the booth after the waitress leaves. "Just to clarify, this is not our real date."

I snort. "I kind of got that when you referred to it as a 'pregame.' Plus, I'm paying for this one since you refused any of the money from our winnings."

He grins. "I'll allow it, but only because you insist."

As we wait for our food, the conversation drifts to lighter topics—college life, mutual acquaintances, and the absurdity of the party we just left behind. It's easy, natural, like we've known each other for more than just a few hours. Which, technically we have on a less personal level, but we've never spoken like this before. It makes me wonder what might have happened had we connected before tonight.

The food arrives, and we dig in, the exhaustion catching up to me with every bite. Still, there's a warmth in my chest that I can't quite explain—maybe it's just me coming down from the high of the night's events, or maybe it's simply from sitting here with Grant. Maybe all of the above.

"I still can't believe I did the challenge," I admit between bites.

Grant looks at me, his expression thoughtful. "You know, most people would never have the guts to do something like that. It takes a certain kind of bravery... or maybe insanity."

"Probably both," I say, laughing. "But that puts you in the same boat as me. Is it weird that I don't regret it? In a weird way, it felt... liberating, I guess."

He nods, understanding in his eyes. "Sometimes you have to do something crazy to feel alive."

"Yeah," I agree, leaning back in the booth. "I guess that's it."

The meal winds down, and we linger over the last few sips of coffee. Despite the exhaustion weighing on me, I'm reluctant to let the night end. There's something about Grant—something easy and unforced—that makes me want to keep talking to him, to keep this connection alive.

When we finally stand to leave, I feel a pang of disappointment that the night is coming to an end. But there's also excitement—a spark of anticipation for what might come next.

"Thanks again for the ride," I say as we walk back to his car. "And the pregame date." The air is even cooler now, and I wrap my arms around myself, shivering slightly. The sky will be starting to lighten soon, and I want nothing more than to collapse in a warm, cozy bed.

"Anytime," he replies as we slip into our seats. He drives with one hand casually on the steering wheel, and when we reach a red light he looks over at me with a playful glint in his eyes. "So, what do you think? You gonna participate again next year?"

I laugh, though it sounds weak with my exhaustion. "Doubtful. Though maybe it depends on how our real date goes."

Grant's grin widens. "I'll take that as a challenge."

As we drive off into the early morning, I can't help but feel an odd sense of satisfaction. Tonight was insane, intense, and completely out of character for me—but it was also one of the most exhilarating nights of my life.

And as I glance over at Grant, I know that whatever comes next—if it's with him—it's going to be one hell of a ride.

Made in United States
North Haven, CT
05 September 2024